Turning Point

THE SEQUEL

A Novel

By: Yasmine Harrison

Turning Point

Copyright (c) 2009

ALL RIGHTS RESERVED

Cover Art by: Yasmine Harrison

ISBN: **145-38-323-78** Soft Cover

FOR INFORMATION CONTACT: Yasmine Harrison at: yasminewrites@yahoo.com or at www.yasmineharrison.com

The Harrison Group

3007 Panola Rd Ste. 109

Lithonia, GA 30038

Printed in the USA

Turning Point

THE SEQUEL

My Dedications

This book is dedicated to My lovely Grand-mothers, My Mother, My Sisters, My Aunts, My Best-Girlfriends and to all of those that supported my first project. (R.I.P Susie Epps, Sadie Harrison, Le'June Reid and Hattie Bonds. I love you.)

A Special Thank You

I would like to Thank God for blessing me with the gift to write and complete this project. Thanks to everyone who put time and effort to help me. Thanks to all my family and friends for your love and support *you all are the best!*

Much Love****Yasmine

4

Turning Point

THE SEQUEL

Embrace your fears, Accept your faults but don't let them consume you. Fall in Love, Be Loved, Give Love unselfishly. Challenge yourself to be the best "YOU", discover your destiny and soar into your future......evolving toward your Turning Point.

~Yasmine~

Turning Point Part II

What A Day

Sobbing and crying, Daya sat in the powder room of the chapel with a cherry wood, chair pressed tightly up under the door knob. She could hear all the chaos on the other side of the door, but blocked it all out. She had never imagined that on her wedding day that there would be three men wanting to marry her. She knew she was fine, but damn. There she sat, in the white iron vanity chair, dressed in her ivory, silk Vera Wang original wedding gown. Taking a deep breath, she went down memory lane. First she thought of Kenyan, she had totally under estimated him. He was much younger, but well on his way to being the perfect man she so desperately dreamed of, but was he ready to give her all that she deserved and desired at this age? Secondly, she thought of Devon. He was so far removed from her life, but seeing him did just spark a flicker not a flame and she was so uncertain about his actions, not to mention the fact that he was very selfish. He was known to pull a whodini act in a heart beat like "poof" and did he reappear to disappear? What was he afraid of and what was he running from or to. Leaning the back of her head up against the mirror, she looked down at the beautiful seven carat titanium ring. Twisting the ring around her finger she, took a deep breath and sighed then her thoughts came to Light. Over everyone else's voice she could hear his. That was so like him not to lose his cool at a time like this. She smiled. She thought to herself that he was such an amazing man. He was everything she wanted and more, but would he keep her in the dark? Were there anymore secrets and could she trust him with her heart again. Whatever she decided she was going to do it in on her terms. "On my terms."

****

Daya sat in the park watching the young children playing on the merry go-round ride.

"Wow what a difference a year makes." she said sitting on the swing in her orange haltered sun dress, she removed her feet from her gold Coach thong sandals and curled her toes in the sand. As she held on to the swing the sound of her bangles soothed her. Her hair blowing in the slight breeze relaxed her and she went into deep a trance.

Things had happened so fast and she wondered where in the world, all the time went. Taking a sip of her bottled water, she reflected on the previous year.

The **it Hit the Fan

The phone rang just as she was on her way out of the door, headed for Tennis practice. She had taken an interest in Tennis in hopes of sculpting a banging body like Serena Williams. Tennis had become one of her many outlets.

It was the restaurant, one of the chefs and a hostess had called out sick for the night. This was not an inconvenience, but it required immediate attention. She always made sure that they were well staffed. She phoned the replacements and quickly got that squared away. The restaurant Mama Sugar's was doing well and had become a hot spot for tourists as well as the locales. Daya was extremely proud of the success. Fumbling through her purse for her car keys, she found her ring. She had been looking for it for about two weeks now.

"Finally. I've been looking all over for you. There!" She said looking at the ring as she placed it on her finger and held her hand out.

Disturbed by the loud knock at the door. She peeped out the peep-hole. It was the police.

"Police! Shit! Who is it?"

"Dekalb County Police."

"Oh Lordy...What the heck?"

The middle aged gentleman spoke in a very authoritative tone, just as he was trained. He was well dressed in a dark navy suit, black leather square toed dress shoes with matching belt, white shirt, red and navy suspenders, accented with a striped powder blue, red and navy silk tie. He was about 6'2, caramel brown complexion, a neatly shaved bald head, nice broad shoulders and beautiful pearly whites. His hands had a very masculine look, but showed signs of roughness.

"Ah Yes." She answered with hesitation and fear in her voice.

"Good Morning, 'maam. Detective Mallick looking for Daya Young Worthington."

Although she was enjoying the view she thought safety first. "May I see your badge please?" The officer pulled out his badge.

"Oh shit!" Opening the door looking puzzled.

"Daya?" He smiled. Enjoying the view of her sandy brown legs in that short yellow tennis skirt. She had nice thick, toned slightly bowed legs with an ivy ankle tattoo on her ankle. She had gotten it one summer in college. She had gotten it to cover up a childhood scar.

"Paul?" She recognized him from the precinct.

Paul also went to college with her. He was a star athlete, in both basketball and football. He and Daya's paths had crossed on numerous occasions. Paul always had an eye for Daya, but thought she was way out of his reach. During those days he only dealt with women with low self esteem and those that stroked his ego, because he was very insecure.

"Yes, I'm here to follow-up on the investigation."

"Look I told you three weeks ago, I don't know anything' bout any stolen art. RJ bought those pieces and gave them to me as a gift."

She thought to herself. What else was this nigga into? He was on the DL, drugs and now stolen art.

"Yes, ma'am I know that, but I came to tell you that we found Dr. Worthington dead in his home last night. We have you listed as his next of kin and I have a few questions for you."

"What? next of kin. Hold on- hold-on and did you say dead? I need to call my attorney."

Daya phoned Booker T and explained the situation.
He informed her not to say one word.

"Well, Mrs. Daya we are going to have to take you in
for questioning."

"Are you serious? Well I need to make another
phone call."

She phoned Margo gave her the information and
asked her to meet her at the police station and to call
the others. Margo didn't call a soul. She jumped in
her black, H2 Hummer and drove it like; she was a
solider at war dodging bullets.

On the way to the precinct, she thought to herself of
all the people in the world why would they contact
her. She had not seen or heard from RJ in over a
year. Why would someone want RJ dead?

The interrogation was more than she could handle
they really were trying to pin RJ's death on her, but
Booker T was not having it. He stuck it to their asses
like, bubblegum on the bottom of a shoe. Daya was

proud of his work. She knew that without a shadow of a doubt that he would not let her go down. After he finished with them they were singing praises to Daya. He ripped those detectives a new asshole. Daya walked out there with her head in the air.

"They had you going for a minute huh?" Booker T said with a real serious look on his face, then scratching his chin.

"Hell yeah! I was waiting for you to jump in. I thought that you were going to let them eat me alive."

Smiling and then breaking into laughter. "You know that I was not going to let them touch one hair on your pretty little head. I had to see what they were working with. I wish you could have seen the look on your face." said Booker T.

She hit him slightly on the shoulder. "You're a mess!"

"Yeah you know how I do it. Can't go in too strong you gotta let them fuck themselves. Oh! And by the way RJ's attorney called me on yesterday. It appears that he never got around to changing his insurance policy and seems like that RJ had forged a marriage certificate and everything has been left to you my dear."

Daya damn near fell to the floor. Margo and Booker T caught her.

"Whew! girl are you alright?" Margo said in her raspy tone.

"Hold on get yourself together, there sweetie pie, you haven't heard the rest. It appears that your boy was pretty stacked. He didn't have any family, he was an orphan. He was raised in foster care and his foster parents are deceased. He seemed to be pretty fond of you because he left everything to you."

Daya could not believe what she was hearing. Shaking her head and sitting down on the light colored wood bench in the precinct hallway. She looked at Booker T, like he was crazy or he had two heads or something. But she knew that he would not lie to her.

"Damn! So that means that I gotta bury him? That motherfucker is still bothering in his death."

"Daya that would be the right thing to do." Margo said looking very serious and motherly.

"Yep! I'm afraid so baby girl. You know you do things in your on time. No need to rush."

They said their good-byes. Margo took Daya home. On the ride home they road in total silence. Daya had a lot on her mind. She was speechless and puzzled. For the life in her she could not understand why RJ would go to such great lengths of forging a marriage certificate.

They pulled in the drive-way.

Margo asked, "You alright? You want me to come in?"

"No, no I'm fine. I'll be alright. I just need a little time to myself. Thanks though."

They hugged and Daya got out the truck.

Margo rolled down the window and yelled loud enough for the whole neighborhood to hear. "IF YOU NEED ME CALL ME."

Looking embarrassed, Daya held her hand up indicating she was fine, unlocked the door and went inside.

As soon as she was inside she fell to the floor. She just let it go. She cried hysterically. It was as if everything she had been experiencing came crashing down on her at once. She consoled herself and got it all out.

She gathered her things and decided she would go for a drive. She felt like she needed to clear her head.

Spilling the Beans

On the drive to nowhere Daya was in such
amazement and disbelief, that she ended up at
Brandy's house. Pulling in the parking deck. She
phoned Brandy.

"Hey chick are you home?"

"Hey sis what's up?"

"I'm on my way up."

"Ok cool!" Brandy said in a chipper voice. She
looked at the phone and immediately knew
something was wrong. She thought that Daya
sounded kind of strange, but would wait for her to
solve this mystery. Then she remember that she had
company and had to usher him out the condo quick,
but before she could get buddy out Daya was at the
door.

The sound of the door bell ringing startled Brandy. She jumped. "Damn! I didn't know that she was literally outside the door."

Opening the door with a big smile on her face and a joke ready to roll off her tongue. She immediately saw that Daya was in distress. Placing her hair behind her ears, she spoke with concern.

"Oh my goodness what's wrong honey?"

Daya didn't answer at all. She swiftly walked pass Brandy plopped on the white leather sectional and made herself comfortable. Brandy stood there with the door open.

"Dang! what's got your panties in a knot?" Brandy blurted.

Sitting on the white leather sectional sofa, accented with custom made turquoise and orange pillows. She glanced up at the chocolate, silk floor to ceiling panels; they really popped against the brick accent wall. Mia had really out done herself; Brandy's condo was definitely magazine ready and was going to be viewed on the home show.

 Daya made herself comfortable and removed her shoes placing them on the chocolate shag rug, which laid in front of the sofa on the concrete floor. Looking out the window Daya folded her arms and viewed the busyness of the city. Brandy walked over and sat next to her.

"Ok tell me what's up?"

Sighing and taking a deep breath. "Girl its RJ he's dead."

"What?"

"Yes, girl and they were trying to put it on me."

"No!"

"And to top it off he left everything to me."

"Damn Day again. Why everybody die and leave you money?"

Daya looked at her sideways and smacked her lips.

"Ok, I'm sorry. So what are you going to do?"

"Girl, I'm going to cremate him and have a memorial. I have to do the right thing. Shit!"

"Okay, if there is anything that I can do let me know."

"Girl, you can start by pouring me a glass of wine. This has been one crazy morning."

Brandy got up and walked to the kitchen. Then this fine ass milk chocolate brother comes out of her bedroom with no shirt on wearing his gym shorts.

"Oh! damn baby, I didn't know that you had company."

It was Norris Walnut the superstar actor. He looked even better in person and from where Daya was sitting he was in 3D. He was chiseled; every muscle was in its proper place. He looked much like a Greek statue.

"I'm not company. I'm her sister and you are…"

Cutting her off Brandy said, "Yes this is Norris."

He reached out to shake Daya's hand. "Pleased to meet you."

"Likewise." She said with a big smirk on her face as she eyed him from head to toe.

Brandy pointed him towards the room. He said, "Ah excuse me for a minute ladies, I am going to go put a shirt on."

"Yeah you do that." Brandy said giving him a who told you to come out here look.

He went back in the room and closed the door.

"Guuurrrrrrrrl!! Girl! Girl he put the smooth in chocolate. He is fine as all get out. I cannot believe how damn fine he is…whew! It outta be a crime. I know that they have a warrant out for his arrest."

"For what?"

"For being so damn fine."

They high fived each other in agreeance.

"Girl say it again…"

"Let me get out of here. This day has just been too much. Sounds like a day for Toinette. I need to let her wash some of these blues away."

Shop Talk

She pulled out her cell phone to call Toinette.

Toinette was her hairstylist and longtime friend.

They had been friends since elementary school.

Toinette could burn some hair honey. She would

have you died, fried and laid to the side in no time.

She was a short brown curvy woman. She always

rocked a fly weave and was hell with the scissors.

She would make you feel like a million bucks.

Besides she was a good listener. She was like a

therapist, but free and without the couch. She would

share her own personal issues and dilemmas, but was

just good to talk too and that is what Daya needed

right now.

"Hey girl what's up?" Daya sounding down.

"Nothing much girl what's going on with you?"

Toinette said with her silver, FHI flat irons in her

hand.

"Girl I need one of those mad head massages a

shampoo and I hope you got some wine."

"How long before you get here?

"Girl give me twenty minutes."

Daya headed to Salon Fretwell's. On her drive there
Mia called.

"Hey chick what's up?" Mia asked full of energy.
"Nothing much just headed to the salon." Daya
spoke in a dreadful tone.

"For real! Girl me too. Good I can share my good
news with you there."

Daya and her friends often met at the salon. They all
loved Toinette and her crew, her assistant
Ki-Ki and especially her male receptionist Q. Ki-Ki
little short, brown big booty could shampoo the heck
out of your head. She was straight as long as she had
her blunt. When she got missing we all knew she
was in her car getting blazed. She was smart as hell
and could mix some fire colors. Then there was that
Q, he was a piece of art. He was about 6'3, with
smooth, delicate sand paper skin. He sported a clean
shaved bald head and had the prettiest white teeth
and smile you ever wanted to see. Homeboy could

hang some clothes and he was sweet. All the ladies loved him because he was always kind to everybody and so attentive. He was divorced and just enjoying the single life for now.

Toinette kept them all fly. She never duplicated a style. It would be similar but not exact. Mia hung-up without saying goodbye. That was strange because she always held you hostage on the phone.

Daya pulled into the parking space next to Mia's champagne 645i convertible BMW.

"I guess she beat me here damn coo-coo bird." She put the car in park grabbed her laptop, purse and headed inside the shop.

To her surprise the whole gang was there minus Brandy she was at home all booed-up with Mr. Finer than fine. They all ran up to her and gave her a hug.

"Hold on. How did all yall end up here? Yall are always up to something." she said titling her head to the side, looking each of them straight in the eye, while dropping her hands on her hip.

Mia ran up to Daya and grabbed her hand. I'm so sorry about RJ, but I gotta tell you something. Come sit down." She guided her to the common area in the middle of the shop. Toinette had the shop laid. It was on a loft style with the brick walls and cemented painted rustic orange and chocolate floors. She had the waiting area in the center of the shop. It was very cozy. She had plush tan colored leather sofas and chairs with oversized sky-blue, yellow, chocolate and orange pillows. She had cream silk floor to ceiling panels with chocolate tie-backs and all the accessories fit perfectly. She had Q posted up in the front. He was a nice piece of eye-candy. The ladies loved seeing him sport his tan Timbs (timberland boots), True Religion jeans with a slight sag and his little shirts that complemented his pecs. He decorated the front well. He was so polite and courteous. He would pamper us to death. He had lips similar to LL Cool J but sexier and was always licking them. It drove the women crazy. He always got pussy thrown at him. The women would size him up and make all kind of offers. But you know who just had to have him right…..Trisha. Yes, she damn near got banned from the salon for having sex with him during and after shop hours. Honey they would be all in the loft area, the laundry room and the break room. Trisha was getting her back broke by Q and loving every minute of it. But this time around things were a little bit different she was paying him. Not that he needed the money because he was stacked. It was funny because you know that she is always trying to get money from men. Q was pimping her big-time. He was an ex- football player and was a silent partner in the shop. He had several other businesses but was just real low-key. He didn't have too many people in his business. But you know Toinette can't hold water. They knew each other from high school and they were always just cool. She would always complain about her trifling husband to him. He would sit quietly and listen to every story.

"Hey Girl!" Toinette shouted from the shampoo bowl as she shampooed Shayla's hair.

She waved. Throwing her hand up.

Daya already knew what Mia wanted to tell her, because Kathy had called her earlier during the week and told her. As a matter of fact they had been talking quite often lately. Kathy had shared with Daya that she was seeing her ex-husband and that they were considering getting back together. She said that she felt like this thing with Mia was a faze and that as soon as the adoption was final she would hastily run back into the arms of her husband. She said she missed everything about him and that they talked about starting a family of their own. She often confided in Daya. It was hard for her because she loved them both.

Daya sat and listened to Mia as if it was her first time hearing the news. She acted surprised and excited and even came to tears as if she was so overjoyed.

She deserved an Oscar or an academy award for this performance. What's a girl to do she thought.

"I just want to let you know that you are going to be an aunt." Mia said sitting there looking at Daya like a proud expecting mother.

"You're getting invitro? 'Cause I know yall you know…" Daya said trying to look puzzled.

"No we are adopting. We are getting a little girl and her name is Olivia." She smiled and waited for a response.

"Oh wow! That's great! When?" she asked.

"Little Ms. Olivia will be ours in about a week." Sticking her chin up she smiled and patted Daya on her hand.

"I can't wait to meet her. I'm going to be the best Auntie." Daya said proudly.

She really was excited about the news, but did not want Mia to crash and burn once Kathy hit her with the news that she was leaving and going back to Mitchell. Mitchell was Kathy's ex husband; he was a pretty cool guy. He wasn't the most attractive person in the world but he had a body out of this world. Nothing to run home and tell mama about. He was definitely fine as hell. Working out was his religion. He worked-out faithfully every single day. He was very sweet and had a nice personality, but he was no push over and when he finally put his foot down Kathy couldn't handle it. She had pushed the poor man over the edge and all that nice shit went south, and then he became hell to live with.

Mitchell was as dark as the night, on the darkest winter night. He was about 6'1, bow legged, nice shoulders and back. He was cut nice. He wasn't making a whole lot of noise but he was fine and good hearted. He loved Kathy to death and gave her anything her heart desired, but she was very hard to please. The more he gave the more she wanted and the more unappreciative she became. But nowadays, things between them were starting to pop off again. He knew about Mia, but was not at all threatened by her or their relationship. That's why every time he and Kathy got together he put it on her. He beat that thang like he was making a cake and that just drove Kathy crazy. She knew that her and Mia could only do so much in the bedroom with their toys and all of their creativity had ran out. But homeboy had come back with a vengeance. He had Kathy feeling like she had died and gone to heaven. They sparked something that they didn't seem to have in their marriage the first time around. This time they took time to really get to know each other and to understand and respect one another. She told Daya that this was the happiest she had been in while. They decide that they would take it slow and let things develop in time.

Daya had had an earful. You know Mia could talk besides she was excited and going on and on. Daya was praying for Ki-Ki to call her to the shampoo bowl, but she was not moving fast enough. She rested her head in the hand. She was overwhelmed with the events from earlier. She zoned out and start thinking about who would want RJ dead. Why did he leave everything to her and not Chaka? She could not believe that he did not have any family. She thought about his service and what would she say or do. She thought damn how did I get mixed up in this. She cried out silently "Lord explain this one."

This was weighing heavy on her heart. She motioned for Q, waving her hand for him to come in her direction. He was walking around with glasses of moscato. She wanted to make sure he didn't forget her. When he got to her she downed her glass and whispered, "refill please."

Q starring at her like she was crazy said "Are you alright?"

"Yes, I mean.. No, but I will be."

He walked to the kitchen to retrieve another bottle of wine and brought it to Daya.

"Here! Look like you need this." Laughing he looked at Mia.

"Let me help you." He said looking at Daya, then started massaging her shoulders.

Daya thought to herself "damn this feel good...this brother got mad skills." She closed her eyes, leaned back and for a moment forgot where she was, then she heard Ki-Ki loud mouth calling her, but she didn't answer.

"Daya..Daya...damn! Daya are you getting your hair washed or what? Or did you come for Q?"

He then began to massage her head. Mia sat there looking like she wanted a massage, but glanced over at Kathy. Kathy rolled her eyes and gave her and I don't care look.

Mia called Daya's name, " Daya..Daya girl Ki-Ki is waiting for you."

Immersed in her massage she opened her eyes with all eyes on her with a big smile on her face, looking like she just had an orgasm.

Shayla sitting in Toinette's chair said "You might want to check your panties 'maam."

Everybody busted out into laughter. Daya looked shame, because she did feel a little wetness between her legs, but she would never admit to it. In all honesty when Q massaged you, you damn near had a multiple orgasm. He had away with his hands, he really made your body relax and he knew the right touch points.

She got up to walk to the shampoo bowl with her legs feeling like spaghetti. Trying to play it off she tried to stretch. Everyone knew what time it was, because they had all been under the hands of Q.

The day at the salon was much needed, it was both relaxing and rejuvenating. It gave her time to regroup, get her thoughts together and think about what she was going to do about RJ.

She and the girls left the salon and went to Houston's on Peachtree. That was one of their favorite hang-out spots. She phoned Brandy to invite her but her, but she was attending a function with Norris. This was really revitalizing because, she had decided to venture into acting and was doing well in her classes and had landed a few small roles on some TV- sitcoms, but her ultimate dream was the big screen. She had been offered a few roles, but felt that she was not ready and would not step-out half stepping

Hanging Out

They all arrived at Houston's, Shayla had beat us
there and was sitting at the bar, having a drink and
conversation with this fine ass white guy. He was
breath taking. He had the prettiest blue eyes you
would ever want to look into, dark brown-hair, the
deepest dimples and most gorgeous teeth and smile
ever. He was dressed in a neatly pressed, nice white
cotton button down shirt with blue stripes, some dark
denim jeans and brown loafers. He wore his shirt
outside his pants for a sporty rugged look. He had a
scruffy but neat beard and a low hair-cut.

When we walked in she didn't see us. You could tell
they were having a good conversation. They were
both smiling, laughing and given the other their
undivided attention. Kathy walked over to inform
her that we had made it and were about to be seated.

"Excuse me. Hey girl! I just wanted to let you know we're here and about to be seated."

" Oh..ok, I'll be over in a minute. Kathy this is Scotland."

He stood and extended his hand. "Pleased to meet you."

"Likewise." Kathy spoke checking him from head to toe. She looked at Shayla smiled, winked and walked back over to the waiting area. She informed the hostess that they were ready to be seated.

At the table we all quizzed her as normal.

"Well who is that she all wrapped up in a conversation with?" Mia asked.

"Yeah, she supposed to be meeting us up here but she all over there with some white dude."

Daya remarked rolling her eyes folding her arms, then looking in the direction of the bar.

"Look, yall need to ask her all that when she comes over here. All I know is he is a fine ass white boy." Rolling her head, smacking her lips and giving them a stiff look.

Shortly afterwards Shayla joined them at the table and the questions flew like nets to fresh shit. She could not place her napkin on her lap for all of them were very inquisitive and could not rest until they had the 411 on the mystery man at the bar.

Shayla was delighted to see that the girls were sweating Scotland hard. Not only was he handsome he was fine. Scotland Philemon was his name. He was 6'3 with blue eyes, brown hair and a nice slim but muscular frame. It was very obvious that he worked out and was in shape, because his shoulders and arms were very defined. He had olive under tones. He was very sexy.

Shayla's mouth ran like water from a broken pipe. She began to tell her girls how they met.

"We walked into the restaurant together he held the door open and told me that I was just as beautiful as my hair. He asked if I was alone? I told him that I was waiting on some friends. Then he asked me if I had time for a drink. Knowing yall slow asses. I said yes. We talked had a very interesting conversation, he asked me out, I said yes, we exchanged numbers then yall came there."

" Oh honey! he is fine as all get out. Girl, I know you 'aint going to let that get away." Laughing and giving high-fives Daya replied.

In agreement they all shook their heads and looked at Shayla.

"What?" She said shrugging her shoulders and looking them all directly in the face.

"Well, he looks a hellava lot better than that damn monster Bruce." Mia replied snickering and waiting for back-up. She knew that she was treading on thin ice talking about Bruce. Kathy jumped in to rescue her. "He sure does! and that's the God heaven truth."

Everyone at the table busted out into laughter. It was definitely true and too funny.

" Why you had to put God in it silly?" Daya said smiling.

"Because God is the truth and he sure is ugly...damn!" Kathy said.

They all busted out laughing again, this time Shayla joined in because she knew that there was no denying his looks.

The server walked up to the table, and interrupted the laughter. A medium height, light brown skinned female, dressed professional and neatly in her black.

" Hi ladies, my name is Ciara. I'll be your server this afternoon."

Leaning to one, side with the order pad in her right hand and the pen in her left.

"Before I get started I have to inform you ladies that your meals have already been taken care of by the gentleman sitting at the corner of the bar."

They all looked in the direction and it was Scott. He nodded and took a sip of his drink. Shayla smiled, winked and held her drink-up. The others mouthed "Thanks!" and waved.

They ordered and enjoyed dinner and drinks. As usual they were laughing, joking, teasing and enjoying each other's company. In the middle of dinner Kathy's phone rang. She excused herself from the table and walked outside. When she returned she advised us that she would be leaving. It was Mitchell. She had forgotten they were supposed to meet at his place. She quickly gathered her things to leave.

Mia asked, "Hey! Where are you in a rush too?"

Thinking of something quick she responded "Oh! it's work. I forgot we had a meeting with some recruits.

Daya looked at her trying not to show that she knew that she was lying. It was a pretty good cover-up though. I don't know how long she had planned to keep this up, but Mia was going to pick-up on this real quick. She was very smart and not so much into the adoption that she was not paying attention to all of Kathy's disappearing acts.

Everyone said goodbyes to Kathy.

"So when are you going to bury RJ?" Shayla asked looking at Daya, wiping her mouth with the linen napkin and taking another bite of her smoked Salmon.

Daya had not even thought about that at all. She had blocked that from her thoughts that quick. The question brought her back to reality. Scratching her head she thought to herself. "Damn!" then responded, "You know I haven't thought about it. In all honesty I forgot about it. I mean to tell you the truth it's not something I'm looking forward to."

Everyone at the table just looked at her. Mia always being the first to reply.

"Girl just go ahead and get it over with. The longer you wait the more you are not going to want to deal with it...Just do it Day. If you want, you know we'll help you." Mia spoke with a sincere voice and catholic nun look.

They all agreed. Nodding their heads in agreement.

The girls enjoyed each others' company. They helped Daya make funeral arrangements for RJ. She wanted it to be over as soon as possible, so she was pleased to know that Shayla made a few phone calls and had everything taken care of before they left the restaurant.

"Wow! Ladies how can I ever repay you?" Daya said looking at each of them with appreciation in her eyes.

"That's what friends are for." Trisha said tapping Daya on the hand.

The next day the funeral service was pleasant, simple and straight to the point. As promised they were all there to support Daya and she was ever so thankful. To express her gratitude she arranged for a weekend road trip to Destin Beach Florida. After the service she informed them. They were thrilled.

Road Trip

It was Friday morning bright and early, they were just crossing the Alabama line. Daya woke them all up at four in the morning for the trip.

"Shoot! Are we there yet darn. I gotta use the bathroom." Trisha said from the back seat wiping her eyes. Lazy butt was not going to drive not one mile. She went to sleep as soon as she got in the truck. Mia had volunteered to drive, her black Expedition XL. It was very roomy. She and Daya sat in the front listening to music and laughing. They went down memory lane, from high school to college. They were laughing and talking until Trisha big mouth woke up. It was good to finally get away. This trip was small but was much needed. Actually, they were taking a trip kind of early this year due to the circumstances. Daya owned a condominium in the area. She had arranged for a spectacular weekend for the girls full of shopping, spa treatments and had hired a chef for the weekend. She had spent big money to make this weekend just what she planned spectacular. Trisha was well on her way to ruining it, with all her gripping and complaining. But she was not about to let that happen. Daya quickly put a lid on that drama. She was hell bent on making this the best weekend ever.

They arrived to the five bedroom, beach front penthouse tired and hungry. The panoramic view was amazing. It displayed miles of powdery, white sandy beaches that instantly relaxed you.

Finley the chef was in the kitchen preparing homemade sweet rolls, seafood omelets, grilled Tilapia, fresh fruits and fresh squeezed juices. It was more than enough to satisfy their appetites.

Daya had each of the girls baskets made with some of their favorites and a touch of hers. They were really elated. Daya really knew how to entertain and loved making her friends happy.

"Daya you got some loot girl! I didn't know your butt was balling like this."

Trisha said licking her fingers and taking another bite of her sweet roll.

As usual Trisha was saying something she had no business. Daya rolled her eyes at Trisha. Mia was not holding her tongue. She cut Trisha done like she was a wild weed in a garden.

"Look here! Don't you start. We are not going to put up with your junk today so cool it! Chick."

She said pointing her finger, with a stern look on her face like she meant every single word. There was complete silence at the table. Everybody looked at Trisha, she looked like a child who had just been reprimanded in the worst way, by her mother and was dared to say a word. She got the picture and got her butt in line.

"You know you always gotta try and start something." Shayla said shaking her head in disbelief at Trisha.

After being roasted she didn't peep a word.

Chef Finley broke the ice, because it was very cold in the room. With his thick French accent he spoke.

"Would you ladies like some fresh hazelnut coffee?"

He came to the table and pored each of them a cup of fresh brewed Bahamian coffee. The coffee was delicious and quite settling.

The ladies each went to their rooms showered and got ready for the beach. Once they were ready they all met in the living-room, beach-wear ready with their swimsuits, designer sunglasses, beach bags, flip-flops and stilettos.

"Hold-on, Hold-on." Shayla said waving her hand.

"Daya now where do yall think yall going with some damn stilettos in the sand? Yall fools gone break your ankles trying to be cute."

They all fell to the floor hysterically laughing. Mia and Daya was trying to be fly.

They had their own fashion show in the living room. They were laughing acting silly like they were teenagers.

Finley was in the kitchen having a field day watching them. Lola, the house keeper had cleaned the kitchen and Finley was preparing lunch, homemade crab cake sandwiches, sweet potato fries and fresh spinach, cole-slaw, key-lime pie, brownies with strawberries and lemonade. He was something else in the kitchen. The food was superb.

He had even prepared them a little something for the beach. After enjoying the fashion show, he was able to get Daya's attention.

"Here, Mrs. Daya, I prepared you ladies a little something for the beach." He said as they were on the way out of the door. He handed her a brown wicker woven basket. It was nice and sturdy. He had it neatly packed with fresh fruits, chicken salad, whole wheat crackers, assorted cheese cubes, napkins, plates and ice cold bottled water. He even had the mints and the ice packs to keep everything cold.

"Gee thanks Finley that was so kind of you."

"Well, just doing my job! Mrs. Daya you're paying me well to take care of you this weekend. So, I'm going to do my best to make you happy."

"Well you are doing great!" She said with a big smile on her face, expressing the fact she was pleased with his services, as she exited the door. She turned back. "I'll call you on our way up."

"Ok. Great!"

A Day at the Beach

On the way to the beach, they stopped by the infinite pool to get their feet wet. Daya had rented sun-chairs, recliners and umbrellas for them.

The attendant met them to assist them with their bags and directed them to private area reserved for them. Daya had big money and loved spending it. Especially on her family and friends. She loved to make them happy.

"Good Morning Ladies, my name is Chico I'll be your personal attendant today. The jet-ski's will be her in about ten minutes and the masseuse's will be here at noon. Can I get you anything?"

"Yes, the time please." Mia said politely.

"Ten thirty, my love." replied Chico.

He was a very tanned, tall and buff young man. He appeared to be about twenty-four or twenty-five years old. He was quite handsome. He was sporting a little sag in his khaki Polo shorts, his shoulders supported the Aqua resort shirt well, giving enough room for his pecks to peep out just a tease. He had nice legs, they were bowed with a tattoo of a cross on his calf. It was evident that he worked-out, because he was in damn good shape. He kinda favored Tiger Woods. He was a sexy little tender. Chico got a little fidgety because he could feel all of their eyes on him and could hear the mumbling. He was certain they were speaking about him, so after getting pass the uneasiness he put on a little show for them. He began flexing his pecks and turned to the back to give them a better view of his derriere. They loved every minute of it. They didn't blink for fear of missing the view.

Flirty women were no problem for him, he had received numerous of propositions working at the resort, from female and male residents both young and old. But he pretty much enjoyed, the company of the older women. His parents owned the resort and he worked there during his off season. He loved the beach.

"Oh we don't start drinking 'til ten thirty-one." Candi said and they all started laughing.

The sun was sitting right on the beach. It was early and very hot. Chico removed his aqua resort shirt for relief, underneath he was wearing a white wife beater. It exposed his nice bulging arms, washboard, back and waistline.

Daya enjoying the scenery spoke, "Damn! P90X and milk does a body good. Tyrese aint got nothing on that. Whew!"

Everyone's attention instantly went in his direction.

Nodding in agreement Trisha said, "Girl you 'aint never lied."

They all joined in laughing, giving each other high-fives.

Brandy sarcastically spoke, "I mean he's alright. He aint got nothing on Norris though."

"Hold on, Hold on! Norris is fine and all but homeboy is definitely competition." Replied Daya.

"Competition shit he is in the race and winning right now. Did you check out the pearly whites, with the dimples, the v- shape from the back, the gluteus, the arms and shoulders? Can we just say he is super HOT!" Mia spoke with confidence and snapped her fingers.

Everybody looked at her with a stunned look on their faces.

She quickly responded, " I might be in a lil situation and all, but I do know fine when I see it. And that's fine."

They went back and forth making fun, laughing and talking and teasing each other.

Daya tuned them out and went into her own zone. Sitting there in her turquoise and gold two piece, catching a few rays and getting her tan on her thoughts got away from her, all she could think about was RJ and Paul. She thought to herself, the nerve of them both, that damn RJ done went off and got himself killed by God knows who and the nerve of that damn Paul. I dare he try and put the shit on me then go try and slide me his number on a sly. I'll bust him in his head. Gone try and lock me up then try and get a date with me in the same breath. Oh! Nigga please. Just the mere thought of RJ made her skin cringe, but at the same time she felt sorry for him. She could not believe that he had actually forged a marriage certificate and left every penny he had ever worked for and stolen to her. He was actually a train wreck waiting to happen. His story was kind of sad, when you think about it. He was an orphan no blood relatives to his knowledge. He clung to Chaka and her family like glue because they were the only ones that he felt like treated him like family. He was a scholar. Brilliant in every way he achieved many accolades in college and in his profession. Graduating at the top of his class from Morehouse medical school and known as the best in his field. But there was a certain emptiness inside. He craved love and affection. He was always trying to achieve acceptance.

Vanished in the movement and the relaxation of the ocean, Daya drifted off to sleep. RJ appeared in her dream, he was talking to her telling her how much he loved her, how much he missed her and how sorry he was and asking for his forgiveness. She woke up to Shayla shaking her. "Girl, girl! Wake-up! Wake-up! You're crying."

Looking puzzled Daya responded. "Crying!"

She sat up and tried to get her composure together. Looking around trying bring back to her memory where she was. Then it donned on her that she was dreaming.

They all came and sat around her chair. Mia handed her some water, "Boo are you ok?"

Breaking a smile through her rapidly beating heart, nodding her head she answered "I'm ok. I'm ok."

Wiping the sweat from Daya's forehead Trisha said, "Day get yourself together. It's alright."

Come on yall let's take a walk on the beach, Brandy said.

They took a stroll on the beach holding hands. No one spoke a word until Daya broke the silence and told them what she had dreamt about. They all did a big sister hug and fell on the ground laughing.

Daya spoke through her laughter, "yall are so stupid."

They sat on the beach for a while and talked. Then this fine Caucasian bow-legged man came running down the beach, with some yellow shorts and a tight white t-shirt with some brown Calvin Klein shades. As he got closer. Shayla thought to herself, I know those legs.

The mystery man approached them and spoke.

"Hi ladies! Shayla?"

"Scott?" Shayla said acting surprised. Trying to play it off like she didn't know he was going to be there. Knowing all along that the two of them had planned this encounter. When she told Scott about the trip he wanted to come, but she told him that she couldn't just invite him on a girls trip. She explained that it was not cool and that the girls would not let it go down like that. So he inquired, " Well what would happen if I just showed up?"

"Not sure, we'll just have to see what happen."

So when she saw him on the beach, she immediately went into actress mode. I'm sure she would have won an Oscar for her performance.

" Wow! Oh my goodness Scott whatta..what a surprise." She said as she gave him a big hug.

He whispered in her ear, pretending to give her a kiss. "You're really over doing it."

She patted him firmly on the back to indicate, don't mess it up.

He smiled. "Where are you staying maybe I can take you all out for dinner later."

Shayla looked around and they all agreed with a smile.

Holding his hand, "So, dinner it is." She said brightly.

Standing there looking finer than ever, his smoky blue eyes illuminated in the sun. His shorts hung perfectly on his newly tanned bowed legs. He rested his free arm on his waist and the other around the lower part of Shayla's waist, holding her as if she was his. You could really see her heart smile, it was displayed in her eyes. Bronzed by the noonday sun, she looked stunning in her yellow two piece swimsuit, with the gold multi-colored sarong wrapped around her waist, tied in a knot to her left side, since she was right handed. Her silky wavy bob placed perfectly behind her pierced ears that housed her 18kt gold diamond, David Yurman original earrings.

After making plans for dinner with her friends.
Shayla and Scott walked down the beach hand in
hand. They others looked on admiring the new
couple, until they were out of site.

Daya didn't breathe a word, but instinctly knew that
they had planned this encounter. She smiled to
herself and thought: "Now just who did they think
that they were fooling with this fake encounter."

Trisha always thinking that she is the apple of some
man's eye had the audacity to come out her mouth
and say, "Did any of yall see how he was staring at
me?" as she twirled in her blondish-brown curly hair,
trying to look innocent, which we all knew she
wasn't. She would sex the hole in a door knob, if she
thought she was gonna get some money. She was the
type of woman that found it a challenge to try and
get a man that was already taken. She thought that
she could have any man that she so desired.

I can remember one year in college, at Freak-Nic this
ball player was staying at the same hotel we were

staying in, the Marriott Marquise. He had plenty of women coming around him all night at the sports bar. As we were leaving he said "Excuse me if you don't mind can I walk you to your room."

Trisha responded, "Sure, I was wondering when you were going to step to me."

"Uh! No harm intended but, I'm not into vanilla baby I like chocolate." He grabbed my hand. I tell you no lie her jaw must have had a 10-ton brick in it, because it dropped to her feet. Her mouth was wide enough for an elephant to take resident. I swear you needed a crane to pick up her lips to close her mouth. It was hilarious, because she could not speak not one word.

Cause in her world she is every man's dream, but not in this case.

Nobody agreed with her that Scott was eying her down. They all just gave her an are you serious look and she got quiet like a kid sent to the corner for time-out.

Daya tuned out all the noise that was around her and became one with the earth. She loved the beach and felt like it was the most relaxing place on earth. There she could unwind, relax and release all that weighed her down and leave it there. She was at peace. This was when she felt the closes to God. The beach was her sanctuary. Thinking about all that she had been through lately overwhelmed her. Tears began to roll down her face, she was broken but not bitter. She knelt to her knees and prayed like never before.

She was concerned as to what direction her life was heading in now, being that RJ's death had just sent her in a tail spin. Along with everything else. Feelings of sadness and disappointment overcame her once again and she cried out unto the Lord. She prayed and asked God for relief, direction and peace. As she was ending her prayer her cell phone vibrated. She glanced at her phone it was Light. He'll call back she thought. He left a message, then sent a text. "Dang!" she whispered. Another call came through, it was Paul.

"Don't these brotha's see I'm praying trying to get myself together and get things right with the Lord. Geesh-Louise." She sighed. "Huh!" letting his call go straight to the voice mail as well.

Later that evening, Scott took them to Dangy's restaurant on the beach. His friend owned the joint and was very generous and hospitable. We had a great time, we enjoyed the karaoke and live performance from the band. The food was delicious. We all had more than our share of drinks, but Scott made sure we arrived back safely to condo. Meanwhile he and Shayla headed back to his place for a night cap. So she thought. When they returned to the oceanfront beach house, Scott pulled back the sliding glass doors for the purity of the sound of the ocean to be heard. He grabbed Shayla's hand and guided her out the door. He gently picked her up in his strong masculine arms, that caught her by surprise and she put her arms around his neck for safety, this brought them face to face. They were locked in each others' eyes. He stepped from the porch to the white powdery sand. The beach was literally his backyard. Once his feet were sturdy and secure, he placed her in front of him, with her back to him and wrapped his arms around her. They were both facing the moon. They both gazed at the beauty of the moon and how it rested on the ocean, it appeared to be in arms reach. Enjoying the scenery, the smell of her perfume intoxicated him. Neither breathed a word. He kissed her on her neck and nibbled on her ear. She could not believe how good it felt being in his arms. She felt safe, secure and wanted. In her mind she wished he would take her right there at that moment she wanted to belong to him. He touched her body in all the right places. He knelt to his knees, behind her. Her legs got limp but, he firmly held her thighs. Slightly opening them, lifting her dress to remove her panties and taste her heavenly treasures. She exploded like fireworks on the fourth of July. He enjoyed the sweet taste and festooned her treasure with his lips, making sure that they were very acquainted. He then pulled a magnum condom out of his pocket, slipped it on, picked her up and placed her on top of him. Her handful of breast perked, her nipples rose to the occasion and she felt his manhood inside her which made her feel better than she had felt in a long time. He explored every part of her body. Each time he craved her more than the last. He wouldn't stop until they were both completely satisfied, she had already surpassed that meter but could not stop enjoying him enjoy her.

Back at the condo Daya and the others 'showered and dressed for bed. Something was weighing really heavy on her heart, she was restless so she sat in the wicker chase on the ocean front balcony. The sound of the ocean always seemed to relax her and relaxation was high on her priority list. Laying back on the chase she crossed her hands and placed them in her lap closed her eyes and inhaled the ocean fresh-air. Gazing at the moon she drifted deep in thought. It was at that moment that she had a revelation and it overtook her. She realized that she had been holding on to something's that she really needed to let go. Things like past hurts, disappointments, old relationships, broken relationships all weighed her down and gave her a heaviness that made her a functional griever. She was in grief, but did not know how to let go. So she ran inside got some paper and made a list of the things she wanted to let go. As she was making her list everything seemed to make sense, the reason why she horded her feelings stemmed from her childhood and her father, when he walked out on them she held on to the father she knew and wanted so that became a way of life for her, when people would hurt her or walk out of her life she would still hold on to them never letting go until this very day. She had never realized this. After she finished her list she quietly slipped down stairs to the beach place her list in a bottle and tossed it into the ocean for them never to return. At last she was finally free. Free from all the heart and pain that weighed her down and hindered her destiny. For instance, like Light when he disappeared she could not move on with her life, she was stuck and how angry she was with Mama Sugar for dying and Devon how in the hell did he still have a place in her heart and RJ why in the world was she still holding on to him. It was time to move on and let go of the emotional ties. Tossing her list in the ocean she felt free. All the people, persons, places or things that had her bound were gone.

She yelled and screamed, "I'm free! I'm free! Free to be me!"

A New Beginning

Toinette turned Daya around to look in the mirror. "Here! I hope you like it since you insisted that I cut your hair." They had argued back and forth about an hour earlier about this new look. Toinette wanted to bob her hair, but Daya wanted a short cut similar to Halle Berry. Toinette reluctantly gave in, when Daya threatened to go to another stylist and take a good number of the clients with her. Although she was just kidding around, Toinette wanted to see how far would she go. They both knew the other one love them and that this was relationship was more like a marriage. They would argued, fuss, stop speaking then make-up like nothing ever happened. This was so routine for them. On one occasion Daya wanted color, Toinette said no the color would bring her hair out well Daya did the color herself and the color was beautiful. So, she stopped going to Toinette and started going to some famous stylist and he brought all her hair out trying to put some expensive   treatment on it. Guess where she ended up back at Toinette's. So, today's fight was nothing unusual.

"Girrrrrrrrrllll! I love it! Honey! You bad!" Daya said patting the back of her freshly cut hair. Holding a mirror in on hand and one over her mouth. "OMG! I wonder what...never mind I like it!"

"Oh yeah it's hot! You are rocking it. I was afraid of the cut because you know you got a funny shaped head." She said then busted out laughing tapping her foot on the ground. Daya rolled her eyes then gave her a stern look, pushing her lips up like she just bit a lemon. "That's not funny." Trying not to laugh, because she knew that there was some truth to it. With thoughts of what she was going to do next, Daya looked in the mirror and admired her new look. Smiling and standing behind her waiting for her reaction Toinette stood there with her hand on her hip. They said their goodbye's and Daya headed off to her next adventure which was to get some new make-up and earrings to compliment her new cut.

She had decided that she was even going to catch a session at Te-Te's jazz bar and maybe a little something else if she was lucky. She smiled.

Paul sat there across from his homeboy Brown with his cell phone, in the palm of his hand wondering if he should try and reach Daya again. He was fresh out of a divorce from a marriage that had ended before it began. He had been taking it easy and was fresh back on the dating scene. He had finally conjured up a nerve to ask Daya out.

Brown just looked at him and shook his head, then responded "Man you got some serious issues. I'm trying to tell you dog it 'aint that serious. From what you tell me she is a nice lady man so hustle up some nerve and give the lady a call. Stop acting like a wimp. You wanna talk to her. So call her."

"Man 'aint nothing about me wimpy. I just don't want to seem like a stalker."

Just as he finished dialing her number his phone rang. He was startled. It was her. He would never admit to it, but his heart dropped and he darn near pissed in his pants when he saw that it was her. Looking at the phone he decided to let it ring so that he wouldn't appear over anxious although he was. Newly divorced. He had just ended his second marriage and was not sure about dating, but could not stop thinking about Daya, since he last saw her. He felt bad and wanted to apologize for the interrogation, but work was work. He wondered if she would give him the time of day. He prayed that she would.

"Man answer the damn phone nigga, you gone let her get away." Brown said shaking his head.

Paul gave him a sinister look, smirked then pressed the green send button on his cell phone to answer the call.

Calling a guy was so not like her, but she pretended that she was returning his call. After all

she was looking good and feeling good. So what the
heck, she thought. Then she remember why this was
such a hang-up for her. When she was sixteen, she
spent the summer with Mama Sugar. She had just
discovered how to attract boys with her figure, by
mimicking Mama Sugar. She had her walk down pat
and was not at all shame to show off her dimples.
After begging Mama Sugar to death she finally got to
go to the skating ring with her rival cousin Sue. That
was the night she met Kent, the most handsomest
guy in the whole town. He was every teenage girls
dream. He was a star athlete, tall, fair complexion,
green eyes, jet black curly hair, the prettiest teeth you
every wanted to see, cherry Kool-Aid lips and a
smile out of this world. He had just graduated from
high school and was on his way to college. He had
landed a full scholarship plus stipend from the
University of Florida. A hot commodity he was. He
was raised by his grandparents. The word was as a
teenager his dad a star athlete as well, got the
mayor's daughter pregnant, he was banned from the
town. Back in those days interracial dating was not

accepted. When Kent was born they left him on his Mimi 's doorstep with a note. "Raise your own nigga boy."

Needless to say Kent was everything but a failure he excelled in academics and athletics. Everybody loved him. He had the best personality. He could have any girl in town and all of the neighboring cities, but he was very interested in Daya, but Mama Sugar and his Mimi were rivals they never got along. So for these two to be together they had to sneak around. Word got back to Mama Sugar from one of her talking patrons in the store and she roasted Daya. She told her women don't call men and hung the phone up when Daya was calling Kent.

She said "If a man wants to talk to you then let him call you. Us Young women don't chase men. Men chase us. You hear me child? I don't mind you dating the boy just don't be so available to him. Sittin' round here starring at the phone. Make him chase you. 'Cause you are a gem. You hear me talkin' to you girl? I mean it!"

Nervously speaking after going down memory lane. "Yes, umh hi you called and I'm returning your call."

Clearing his throat he spoke in a deep sexy baritone voice. " Yeah I've been trying to reach you. Nothing related to the case I was wondering if you were available for dinner tonight?"

"I can be. About what time?" she answered hastily, without thinking twice about it.

"Is seven fine?" he asked surprised that she agreed.

"Ok. That's cool." Freely speaking without a care at all.

"I'll pick you up?" he spoke excitedly.

"No thanks. I'll meet you at Surfer's." she answered short of no hesitation. She thought to herself, shit I'm free, but not that free.

"That sounds cool."

"See you then."

Looking at the phone as she hung it up she asked herself. Did I just make a date with this man. She rationed. It's not a date it's just dinner. My husband is going to kill me. She laughed to herself because the words that had just rolled off her tongue sounded weird and were very unfamiliar to her. Shrugging her shoulders she turned up the soft sounds of Joe. She jammed to his easy listening vocals. Stopping at the traffic light she snapped her fingers and bobbed her head to the music. She pulled down the mirror to check out her new look for what seemed like the one thousandth time since she left the shop. Patting and running her fingers over her newly shaved and neatly tapered head, she cracked a smile and once again admired her new look. She was startled by the car next to her blowing the horn. She looked in the direction. There sitting in a convertible champagne jaguar was the most attractive older man she had ever laid eyes on. He smiled, nodded and motioned for her to roll her window down. She did and focused on his beautiful pearly whites.

"Yes." Curiously speaking.

"Hi, there pretty lady. You got a minute?" He spoke confident and not at all challenged.

"No, not really. What you need directions or something?" Trying to rid herself of him, but his charismatic attitude was drawing her in.

"Yea as a matter of fact I do, the way to your heart."

She smiled. "That was cute and original, but seriously I have to go." She began to roll up the window and he asked her to pull over in the Starbucks parking lot. Hesitantly she did. He got out of the car looking like a vision heavenliness. She darn near swallowed her tongue because she could not conceive how attractive this man was. He was about 6'2", with a smooth sandpaper brown complexion, mixed salt and pepper hair that was cut low. He had swagger like Denzel Washington. He was wearing a fresh crisp, white shirt, with the sleeves cuffed up to his elbows, khaki wool blend slacks, chocolate belt with a silver buckle and chocolate loafers. He wore a ½ carat diamond earring in his right ear and a Swiss Army watch on his left wrist. He had a medium build, it was very obvious that he worked out or was once an athlete. He spoke in a deep sexy tone.

"Hi pretty Lady, I'm Collier Bryant."

Extending his hand to her in gentlemanly manner. She kindly accepted his firm but soft well-manicured hand, admiring his fragrance, she smiled and spoke softly. "Please to meet you, I'm Daya."

They exchanged business cards and made plans for lunch the next day.

Her day had become very eventful, but it was the still moments that consumed her. She drove quietly in her car with the sounds of Babyface playing. Smiling as she recapped her encounters, she drove to the mall for new accessories and lip-gloss to compliment her new look. Strolling through the mall and admiring all the latest fashions. She unexpectedly ran into Light. There he stood with his daughter in his arms. Their eyes locked they did not speak a word. Daya turned to walk away and he called out to her, she ignored him and hurriedly exited the store. When she got to the car her heart was racing. Then all that she had been suppressing resurfaced.

For the Good Times

Sitting in the car Daya was in such disbelief. She could not phantom what had just happened. She didn't think that would have been her reaction, but it was. The encounter was not good for her. She was not prepared to face him. He had been trying to contact her, but she avoided him like he had swine-flu.

The truth of the matter was his divorce was never final. He didn't double check the paper work and had never signed it correctly. He signed in the wrong place. Then the day of wedding his ex-contacted Daya to tell her she was pregnant and that she really wanted her husband; although, she knew that he was madly in love with her. He had explained to her on numerous occasions that he didn't love her, but she would not give up. He had told her about Daya and she was envious, denying him an annulment and tampering with the divorce papers. She was determined that he was not going to leave her. Just like she had trapped him into marrying her. That trick Amber was one very conniving spirit.

She had slipped him the date rape pill and had her way with him, even going to the extreme of freezing his sperm. She knew that was the only way she could have him, because once he found out the truth about her he did not want anymore dealings with her. She had even teamed-up with RJ to have him arrested.

Daya took it really hard. She knew that she had compensated for love when Light was away and that no one had ever loved her the way he did and no one ever would. He loved her mind, body and soul and with everything that he had in him. It was all over him. She loved him just the same. The two of them together were magnetic. When they were together their hearts beat as one. You could see the sparkle in their eyes. Anybody could feel the love coming from them because it was strong and forceful. It was like the smell of a finest perfume, it would overtake you consume you, draw you in.

Daya got nervous and busted into a sweat, when she thought about the threat that Amber had made towards Light. Visions of Amber actually carrying out her threat flashed through her head. It made her skin crawl. She was by no means intimidated by Amber and her threats; it was just her history that gave her something to think about. She had been institutionalized numerous times and all her family members had mysteriously disappeared without a trace. Daya had to think long and hard about how she would deal with " Queen Psycho". Her main focus was to keep Light alive.

The soft sounds of Al Green's, "For the Good Times" played in the car. All she could do for now was think about the good times that her and Light had. She thought about how they met and how she knew from the moment she met him that he would be in her life was forever. The many trips and mid-day surprises all the lavish gifts. Then it was the simple things. Yes he was extravagant but, he had a very down to earth side too. He loved every aspect of pleasing Daya. He did it so natural just like blood flowing through his veins. He would always comment that Daya was the beat in his heart. He loved her without malice or guilt.

Light placed his daughter in the stroller and walked to the food court in the mall. He sat there thinking about Daya. He was the happiest he had ever been in his entire life. She was truly special. He was so happy to see her and for her to run off like that hurt him. He had to go and get himself together. Tears whelped up in his eyes because deep down inside he knew that she was his everything and he just couldn't understand why they could not be together. He placed his hands over his face and they absorbed the tears. He rested in that position for a moment, took a deep breath and when he opened his eyes there was the second set of the prettiest eyes he had ever laid his eyes on looking at him cooing. That made his heart smile, but didn't take the hurt away. Joy loved the site of her daddy and he showcased her like his trophy. He was so proud of her. She was such a beautiful baby. Joy was the girl version of him, the spitting image as Mama Sugar would say. She went just about everywhere with him, He didn't feel comfortable leaving her with Amber because she would scream to the top of her lungs and Amber would just sit there.

He picked her up out of the stroller and she grinned from ear to ear with drool dripping on her lavender and yellow bib. He was at the jewelry counter purchasing her some new diamond earrings, then he saw Daya. His heart dropped and he nearly dropped Joy then the store associate caught her. He looked at her discombobulated and said " Here hold her." as he chased after Daya, but she disappeared so fast. Looking into her big beautiful brown eyes he told her "She should have been your mother." He kissed her on the forehead and surveyed the mall for any site of Daya.

Then Trisha walked up.

"Light is that you?" smiling like she just struck gold. She was up to something, you could tell from her demeanor.

Excitedly he responded, "Is she with you?" looking around very frantic.

"Uh Light what..what are you talking about?" she said placing her hand on his shoulder to calm him down.

"Daya she was just here."

"No honey, I'm her alone. What a pretty baby."

"Thanks this is Joy my daughter."

Very flirty, "I see where she gets her looks from." She pulled out a card with her phone number on it.

"Her if either of you need a babysitter I'm always available." She smiled the winked.

He didn't reach for the card, but spoke very vulgarly. " Bitch you know I'm in love with Daya get your skank-ass away from me. I always knew you wanted a peace of me. Listen not every man want easy pussy especially one that has all those miles on it like yours. I always knew you wasn't about shit. Trying to pretend to be Daya's friend, when all along what you really want is to be Daya. You couldn't wait for this opportunity huh? To throw your bait to see if I would bite. Hell no! I peeped you out the first night, I met you, trying to give me the eye. There was no connection then and there is damn sure not one now. You are not my type shawty. Personally, I think its real foul of you." He threw her some cash. "Now go by your ass a self-esteem because you sure don't have one."

She stood there in disbelief. All of Daya's other men would just roll with the game. They had all fallen prey to her sexcapade offers. She truly wanted everything Daya had and secretly envied her success and happiness. Light was an exception to the rule he truly loved Daya and would not ever do anything to intentionally hurt her. He gathered Joy's things placed them in her Gucci backpack put her in the stroller and they exited the mall, leaving Trisha standing right there with her face cracked and on the floor.

A Day of Frolic

It was a beautiful bright scorchering July day.
Artise was having his annual all Pink Affair, in his
garden. He and Frank had worked in the yard
diligently months ahead to prepare for this day.
Artise was such a perfectionist, he had to make sure
the yard was immaculate. He had the house and yard
in pink throughout. He had pink crystal, china,
dinner ware and all. When he did something he really
put his foot in it. I must admit this day was almost as
beautiful as my wedding day. He and Frank had

both straight friends and gay friends. They seemed to always bring everyone together for a good time. Their straight male friends respected their relationship, being that most of them had grew-up together. Can you imagine Artise was an all-star quarterback, homecoming king and an MVP in the NFL. Frank was once a father of two, married to his high school sweetheart. Word had it that he was still messing around with the wife and a woman he was cheating on the wife with Dr. Julie Ackerman. She was way too beautiful to be caught up in this triangle, but obviously not that smart. She could have been a Top Model easily on any day. Tall, black tresses, gorgeous brown skin, nice round full hips the look of a goddess, the confidence of a jellyfish. She was a fragile and shallow individual all she wanted was the company of a fine man on her arms and Frank was just that. She showered him with all kinds of lavish gifts and would give him the world if she had it in her possession. She had darn near though when you think about it. Trips to Dubai, China, and Australia just name a few. She didn't have any children but desperately wanted to have a child by Frank and began taking fertility pills. She had plotted that he or she would impregnate herself on their next escapade. Poor thing she was not aware that he was no longer with his wife and that he had moved on to a same sex relationship, she just valued the time he spent with her. In her mind as soon as he divorced they would be together and live happily ever after.

Not if his wife and Artise had anything to do with it. Honey that wife said that she didn't care how many booty-holes he stuck she was listed on his insurance and was entitled to all his benefits from the military, to his inheritance from his parents and not to mention the fact that she was part owner in the seven stores. She claimed that she had invested too much time in his ass and refused to give him a divorce. She said she would wait patiently for his ass to die. So that she could enjoy the rest of hers.

Artise on the other hand was milking him on a daily basis. Frank had purchased a beach front condo for him on Marco Island then Artise secretly purchased a condo in New York because that was where he had planned to fled to once he had got all he wanted from him. He had always dreamed of entering the fashion world and had solidified some sure contacts. They all were just one hot messed.

The sound of the jazz band set the tone for the party. The ambiance and theme was relaxed and free. Aroma scented candles and tiki-torches filled the air.

It was always interesting to see how the straight men gravitated to one side, how the gay men and the single women conversed and how the married women would sit back and look and analysis everything, getting their gossip on.

Kathy and Mia had been bickering for the past few months you could tell that their relationship was coming to a screeching halt. It was a train wreck waiting to happen. Not to mention that Kathy was three months pregnant and you know it wasn't from Mia.

Artise and Frank were both social butterflies and gave attention to all their guests. From the many laughs, smiles empty plates and wine glasses, it appeared that everyone seemed to be enjoying themselves. It was the scene of the perfect event when all hell broke loose.

It started with Kathy and Mia, because Kathy's husband showed-up, then with Frank and Artise because his wife and kids showed-up, then with Trisha and some woman. She had been messing with the lady husband and had purposely left her panties at their house in the washer and pictures of them in his car over the sun-visor. That lady spotted Trisha from across the garden, she and her friends were pointing and looking in our direction. Within the next few seconds she had slapped the slut out of Trisha. It was as if she dropped out the sky and her hand landed straight upside Trisha's face. She didn't give Trisha enough time to breath her next breathe or respond. She went to work on her, like she was a professional boxer getting paid.

This spectacular day had literally turned into a three ringed circus. The guest now turned spectators did not know which; way to look because altercations were popping up everywhere like ant beds. What started out as an elegantly beautiful day turned into one big chaotic frenzy.

Keep It Movin'

It was a somber day, the day of Kathy and
Mitchell's baby memorial. Kathy had given birth
prematurely and the baby was too young to be viable.
The relationship with her am Mia had severed
months earlier and they were truly a happy couple
again. They had set a date for the renewal of their
vows, but this happened. Sad to say but this incident
brought them closer together and what was meant for
a day of sorrow turned into a day of joy. They
decided that after the memorial they would renew
their vows, but didn't tell anyone they had already
arranged everything and had invited everyone to join
them at the W-hotel midtown for a roof top
ceremony. It was beautiful everyone attended even
Mia. She had told Daya and Brandy that she wasn't
bitter. She guest Kathy was what she needed at that
time and for that time and that that chapter of her life
had been closed. Ironically, that was the day she met
Rylan Houston. She met him in the lobby as she was

headed to her car. He was in town on business from Texas. He was an associate vice-president for a well-known athletic company. He wasn't strikingly handsome but, had a distinctive look about him. He was well dressed in his business attire. A man of tall stature and tall attitude. He was light brown in complexion with a low hair cut. He showed some signs of maturity with the mixed salt and pepper hair. He watched her as she got off the elevator and walked across the lobby. He was taken away by her beauty. He knew that this was a now or never moment. He was swift with his thinking and thought of an easy pick up line.

" Excuse me. Can you tell me where is Peachtree Street?" looking at her never taking his eyes off of her waiting for her to respond. Mia looked around, looked him up and down.

"Are you talking to me?"

"Yes."

"Because you just passed the concierge desk I don't work here." She said and continued walking.

"Ok Miss excuse me I'm sorry I guess that was kind of lame of me, but I just wanted the get your attention and I did." Holding his hand out. " let me start over if I may, I'm Rylan Houston pleased to meet you. I saw you walk across the lobby and thought what a beautiful woman and I just had to come speak. Here!' he said handing her his card.

"Thank you." She said in a cynical tone.

"I don't mean to bother you, but do you have time for a drink?"

"No, no not right now."

"Come on just one." He said smiling waiting for her response then decided he would add. "You really look like you could use a drink and a good laugh if you ask me and I have some funny jokes."

"No funny business let me call my friends and tell them where I'm at and to come check on me.

Mr. Out of town." She said turned and strutted towards the bar area which indicated she accepted the invitation. As a matter of fact she did need a drink, but she was headed home to have one alone before it was time to pick Joy up. Besides it had been a while since she had been in the company of a man and he seemed to be good company for now.

Brandy had started to get nauseated. Her and Brent left. On the drive home he stopped by the local drugstore. He went inside to get a pregnancy test. He didn't tell her until he got back in the car.

"Here." He said handing her the bag.

"What is this?" she opened the bag. "Norris!"

"You've been sick for a few weeks now, what you think I didn't notice huh? Besides you've been sleeping a lot lately." He gave her a kiss on the cheek and they headed home.

Scott and Shayla had delayed their trip to Turks and Caicos for in the morning and decided they would act like tourist and spend the night at the hotel. Things were going great for them. Shayla's practice was growing she had opened a second office and her and Scott were spending a lot of time together getting to know one another and just enjoying being together. It was gratifying to her that he had his own money and that he genuinely appreciated being with her. Bruce on the other hand had been a serious "Bugaboo". He tried to handle Scott like a shorty, but Scott quickly put him in his place and he got the picture.

Trisha didn't make the function she had been laying kind of low since that lady opened a can of whip-ass on her at the party. Seems like "Mrs. I'll take your man" was heading for retirement.

As usual Daya was the last one to leave she wanted to make sure all was well with the couple. Being that she was there solo she was in no rush to get home to be alone. She had phoned the restaurant for a take out order for later. She said her goodbyes and on her way out stopped by the bar to check on Mia. She peeped in it appeared that Mia was in good company. Daya told the hostess pointing in Mia's direction, "If she leaves with him or appears to have had too much to drink or is still here in an hour give me a call." Handing the hostess her card and a one hundred dollar bill. She winked and walked away.

She pulled in the parking lot of Mama Sugar's and there was a nice crowd. She entered the restaurant not like the owner but a patron. She surveyed the restaurant and it was pretty heavy for a weeknight. She walked up to the hostess and asked was everything alright. The hostess greeted her with a big hug all her staff loved her because she treated them well. She gave them insurance, bonuses and vacation. She treated them like family. They all knew that she was strictly business when it came to the restaurant though.

"Hey there sexy lady!" someone said grabbing her from behind. It was Keynan he and some of his attorney associates were having dinner. He had been asking for Daya since he stepped foot on the premises. He was looking handsome as usual just a little older looking. Practicing law had aged him.

"Hi Keynan it's been a while."

"Yeas it has." He said looking her up and down admiring her curves. "I can see nothing has changed with you, you still smelling good, looking good, and riding good you just all good! Ms. Daya."

"Thanks Keynan. So you're visiting?"

"No, I'm back now. I got my own firm"

"Wow! That's great. I'm so happy for you."

"Yeah thank you. Me and my partners you know we eat here on a regular. I was waiting for the moment to run into you."

" Yeah well thanks for your patronage. I appreciate your business."

"Well come on let me introduce you." He grabbed her by the hand and they walked to the table. He introduced her to everyone including his lady friend that was sitting at the table. Daya thought to herself that she looked like a younger version of her. She politely extended her courtesy of paying for the food thanked them for their patronage, checked on the rest of the staff, got her food and left.

On the drive home she could not help thinking that Keynan was dating someone that looked like her. She kind of felt a little jealously. She undoubtly still had feelings for him. The young lady could have easily been her sister. He didn't introduce her as a girlfriend but it was obvious they had interactions inside and outside the courtroom.

An eventful day drove her to emotional eating. She kicked off her shoes plopped on the sofa and dove into her chocolate cake. She was eager to get her hands on the friend chicken, macaroni and cheese, candied yams, black-eyed peas and sweet buttermilk-corn bread. This was definitely a night for two of her favorite movies: "Love Jones and The Notebook". Indulging in the savory of her goodies she ignored the phone ringing for it was in her purse across the room and she was not about to part from her fresh fried chicken. The phone continued to ring and she eventually got up to see who it was. It was nobody other than Margo and Brandy.

She answered so annoyed. "Hello, it better be important."

"Ok why you being smart it actually is." Brandy said.

"I'm going to be a Grandma!"

"We called to tell you I'm pregnant."

"Oh wow! Congrats! That's why you left so early today huh?"

"Yeah Norris bought a test today after we left."

"So how far long are you?"

"Maybe three or four months."

"Months? Ok explain."

" You know I've been filming for the movie and was just stressed about getting the part right and didn't really pay it any attention."

"Girl stop! You hear this Margo?"

"Yea, I hear this mess."

"Well it's possible."

"Well just let me know what the doctor say. I gotta go."

Hanging up the phone she was so excited but the most important thing was her food right now. After finishing her food she curled up in her favorite blanket and fell asleep.

Passing Time

It was not hard for things to pop off between Mr. Collier and Daya. They had been playing phone tag for a couple of weeks and were finally able to coordinate their schedules and confirm a date. He seemed to be pretty persistent and always made a point to keep the lines of communication open. He had great conversation and was always up on the current events.

It was their first date and he invited her to a helicopter ride over the city and a exclusive roof-top dinner prepared by his personal chef on top of his presidential style condominium. Very impressive for a first date she thought. It was noticeably obvious that was his goal-- to impress. Mission accomplished

she thought to herself. Dinner was superb. Chef
Danny Zuto was right on the money with the food.

After dinner they lounged in the cabana
listening to some soft jazz tunes while intellectually
entertaining one another with conversation, a few
laughs here and there, they enjoyed one another like
old friends. He was extremely handsome and very
suave, just like Denzel Washington in *"Mo' Better
Blues"*. He really knew how to treat a lady, he
opened doors for her pulled out her chair, the works.
He had old school mannerism and it was much
appreciated. The evening was maturing and although
Daya was enjoying her self she did not want to wear
out her welcome or give him any mixed signals. She
ended the night and he escorted her downstairs to the
elevator. On the elevator ride down she bumped
into Trisha. She was up to one of her old tricks. She
and an older Hispanic man got on the elevator hand
in hand. She was so startled to see me. Tell you the
truth that girl's heart in is her vagina. She would
hump an ant if she thought she was going to get paid.

When they reached the lobby, they exited the elevator and Collier with a concern look told Daya. " I see your friend in this building quite frequently. She appears to keep the company of many gentleman in this building."

Daya looked at him with her eyes full of curiosity and said " Well has she kept you company?"

With a disgusted look in his eyes he hurriedly responded. "No not at all. Not my type. Besides the miles are kinda high on that ride."

He motioned for the valet driver and he made sure she was safe in her car. She drove off. He walked back in the build thinking how beautiful she was and thought when it would be the right time to tell her he would be leaving to go back to work overseas.

As he entered the elevator his cell phone rang it was Light.

" Hey Pops! What's up?"

" Nothing much son I just had a date with this young tender she kinda put me in the mind of that girl you were telling me about. If I'm not mistaken it's her."

"Daya?"

"Yeah that her name."

"Oh no Pops. Not my baby."

"Hey son nothing happened just dinner. Now that I realize it I'm going to have to tell her."

"Pops you've got to break it to her easy. She's very emotional and she will swear I had something to do with it."

" I told her that I had just reconnected with my son and that I was a grandfather. I'll handle it son. Trust me she will be back in your hands in no time."

"Alright now."

"Hey she's a good catch I don't know how the hell you let her get away."

"This psycho-bitch baby-mama of mine sabotaged our relationship and man I don't know all I know is she is the one and I will do whatever, it takes to have her back in my life. I don't know how I got caught up in this mess with psycho. "

" Well son just rest your mind and we will work on getting your little honey back. By the way how is my grand-daughter?"

"She is doing fine. I gotta go that's her waking up now. I'll get atcha tomorrow. Later."

"Take care Son. Kiss my grand-daughter for me."

Hanging up the phone Light thought to himself that his Pops was kind of smooth for an old man, to have pulled Daya because she was definitely not an easy catch.

Collier grinned to himself as he ended the call. Then he spoke, "That sure is my boy he got my taste in women."

Friendtervention

Every since Mr. Marvin died and she shot Ed
Trisha had been wilding out. She was going through
money and men like water. Daya became very
concerned after brushing shoulders with her in the
Ten-Ten towers and hearing the comment that Collier
made. She phoned Brandy to get her take on it.
Brandy directed her to Mia because she was super
sleepy. Mia and Shayla were both booed-up with
their men so this was one call she was going to have
to make on her own. None of them really liked
Trisha they would always say that's your friend we
just tolerate her because of you. They really didn't
dig a lot of the scandalous stuff she did and how she
would step all over people just to get what she

wanted. I would always tell them that was a cry for help or a sign of insecurity. They would not trust her with a ten foot poll. Mia said she couldn't trust her no father that she could throw her. Mia had her reasons for that because she suspected that Trisha and Howard had something going on but couldn't quit put her hands on it. One evening, at a birthday celebration at my house she noticed that Howard and Trisha both got missing for sometime then she saw him come out the bathroom, in the guest room zipping his pants. Trisha was behind him with this sneaky ass innocent look on her face, from that point on she didn't too much deal with her.

When Daya thought about it Trisha had become very distant lately and had started hanging around a set of groupie looking women. Her appearance had drastically changed she was noticeably slim and had heavy dark circles under her eyes not even makeup could hide. She had stopped messing with Q at the shop and started messing with some flea-bag that was cold blooded pimping her.

Nobody knew nothing about him not even my cousins in the hood or the west-side. My cousin Ta-Ta who was well know in the streets told me that the dude was trouble, but he would get some of his boys on him to find out what he was about.

She had been avoiding my calls when I finally got hold of her she told me she was doing well and doing contract worker but she was straight-up hooking being a prostitute there was no other way to describe it. He had introduced her to cocaine and she was hitting it heavy no wonder she was losing everything she had, the only reason why she didn't lose the house is because it was paid for and I would bet my last dime that she was trying to figure how to get money off that. She let this fool set-up shop in Mr. Marvin's house acting like he built it for his whores. Cobra was his name. Nothing to run tell anybody about. He was just average no keen features no fine body. There was nothing spectacular about him expect for the fact that he had game. He could talk his way into about anything to anyone that gave him the time. He even talked his way into Harvard University for a week, until they discovered that he was not an Asian male name Wong-ho. He preyed on the weak. He was a big time wanna be hustler. He didn't own nothing not even his name he borrowed that along with the clothes on his back, from his cousin who was a real well know drug dealer in Louisiana. His cousin was the real Cobra and he was looking for him because he had stolen money from him. Arthur Declan that was his real name a real nobody from Louisiana.

He washed up from hurricane Katrina to Atlanta. He would rent luxury cars and apartments using fake credit cards until he met Trisha then he just used her big house as his and bought a S500 Mercedes in Mr. Marvin's name. He was as crooked as the lines in the paved sidewalk and he had a grip around Trisha's mind so tight not even the "jaws of life" couldn't free her, but the God in heaven could. Daya had decided no friend of hers was going down not like that. She had to make a decision about how she was going to handle it and fast. She talked it over with the Lord, he gave her an answer and she went with it.

It was in the wee-hours of the morning as Mama Sugar would say. Daya had been sitting in the drive way for thirty minutes praying. It was three a.m. on the dot when she hit the doorstep. She threw anointing oil and prayed all the way up the driveway. She put oil on the front door used her key to go in. She left the door open and yelled to the top of her voice "devil get the hell out of here you have no place here."

She went into prayer. She wasn't no fool now she had the bible in one hand and Clyde in the other. You should have seen the men and women running out of that house. She looked around for Trisha. She couldn't believe how much pride Trisha use to have in this house and how she had let it get run down. The nice pieces of furniture scattered here and there indicated this was once somebody's home and that love did live here at some point. The scene was horrifying. Crack pipes, needles, beer bottles, liquor bottles and used condoms fumigated the place. Daya phoned Ta-Ta for him and his boys to come because one of Cobra's patrons ratted him out by pointing upstairs signifying he was up there. He was a nice looking well groomed man looked to be in his mid-thirties.

"Ma'am I don't want no trouble I'm retired military, I gotta wife and three children. That nigga took all my check. I just wanted a lil' head that's all. My wife cut me off three months ago and my friend told me about this place. Somebody need to stop him because he is scandalous." He whispered in an articulate tone.

"How many people are here?" she asked.

"Oh it's a few upstairs him and his lady and the film crew."

"Film crew?"

"Yeah he got her staring in the movie and he charge forty bucks a head to watch."

"Are you serious?"

"Yep! As a heart attack."

In ten seconds flat Ta-Ta and his boys were there.

"Damn cuz you got here quick."

"Yeah baby girl I followed you. I knew you would try to come over here. I gotta give it to you, you gangster girl. You gotta a lotta nerves coming over her like that by yourself and all." He said giving her a side hug.

" I didn't come alone I brought the Lord and Clyde." Waving her piece and her bible like Aunt Esther on Sanford and Son.

"Whoa! Lil cuz you packing huh?"

"Yep..I guess I learned from the best." She smiled.

Ta-Ta was not really her blood cousin, but they were raised up as cousins and you couldn't tell them no different. His mom and Margo were good friends back in the day but he and Daya always keep in contact. Ta-Ta was a smart as a whip he made a perfect score on the SAT, had a full track and baseball scholarship to a big ten university in Florida. Everybody loved Ta-Ta the young and the old. People flocked to him like flies to shit. He had an amazing personality and people just loved to be around him. The white boys on his baseball team couldn't stomach him being captain and him getting all the publicity and professional contract offers. They set him up and planted drugs in his room and his locker trying to sabotage him, but the charges didn't stick. After that he kind of lost his zeal for sports. He then went overseas to run track professionally, he said he wanted to see a different side of the world and that prejudice wasn't that bad over there. They loved him treated him like gold. He broke all kind of records and went to the Olympics. When he came home he was stacked. He was offered all kind of coaching jobs but decided to stay and coach the inner city kids. He always kept his connections in the hood though. He said he would never forget where he came from. He had a lot of respect with the drug dealers because he stood up to them and wouldn't sell their dope for them when he was younger, unlike some of his friends. Instead of the drug dealers manipulating him he would manipulate them in to buying him clothes and shoes so he could be fresh. He was a smart cat. He talked a lot of them into going back to school and getting off the streets. Some went into the military and some chose the street game. One of his homeboys he got off the streets was Milton Holmes. Milton use to come visit him in college. One weekend he came and never went back. He moved to Florida, went back to high school, graduated, went to college and got drafted to play in the NFL.

So Ta-Ta was affiliated but not affiliated with the streets. He was glad to answer Daya's call when she told him about the Trisha and Cobra situation. He used to have a big crush on Trisha back in the day. She would not give him the time of day because he was younger, but once she saw him all on television and on the Olympics making the big bucks she wanted to holla, but Daya was not about to let that go down. She loved Ta-Ta like a brother and was not about to let Trisha spit her venom on him. Coach TaMarcus Wilkes was his name. He was as handsome as handsome could be. Tall, athletic build, personality out this world, smooth rich chocolate skin, pearly white colgate smile and super intelligent. He was the total package. Ta-Ta had done well for himself. He was an accomplished athlete, coach, son, brother and father. He had fathered a child overseas, but had custody. He was a proud single dad. Looking at him Daya could do nothing but smile because little knuckle-head snotty nose had turned out to be a fine young man.

Being at Trisha's house like this reminded her of back in the day when some boy would get out of line with her she would phone Ta-Ta and his boys and he would be there in no time flat just like tonight.

She looked at the retired military man and pointed him towards the door. The gentleman tried to say something and Ta-Ta reinforced the exit. Ta-Ta's homeboy had phoned the real Cobra in Louisiana and he got on the next plane and was headed to Atlanta. Ta-Ta's homeboys had surveillance and secured the house and was moving in. They broke up the filming upstairs and brought the fake Cobra downstairs in handcuffs. Daya bitch slapped him and asked for the rest of the film. He didn't answer but one the crewmembers told them where all the film was and Daya told them to burn it in the back yard. Ta-Ta's home-boys went to work on him. Ta-Ta told him not to ruff him up too bad because Cobra was on the way and he would handle him.

Trisha was looking a hot mess she was rank and so high she thought she was flying. One of Ta-Ta's homeboys gave her some milk and she stared through up. He said he gave her the milk to get the rest of the drug out of her system.

Daya finished throwing her oil all over the house locked the house up, put up no trespassing signs and took Trisha to her house. Her and Ta-Ta cleaned her up and took her to the drug rehab treatment center. She went shamefully and reluctantly but she needed the help.

Daya phoned for a cleaning crew to go over to the house and clean it from top to bottom.

Mr. Marvin had spoken to Daya some years back and told him about Trisha and drugs. She was just experimenting doing it every now and then. He had hoped that it wouldn't ever come to this point. He told Daya that if anything ever happened to him and Trisha got bad off he knew that he could trust her to be by Trisha's side. He knew how Trisha's butt was and that not too many people really gave a damn if she fell off the face of the earth or not because of her scandalous, conniving ways. He gave her a large sum of money and told her to put this up for Trisha's hard times, because he knew that they were sure to come. It's funny that she didn't give a donkey's hot shit about him but he sure loved her and took good care of her even after his death. Daya pondered on what to do. She knew that Trisha was not stable enough to handle anything and decided that she would give it to her in installments after she completed her ninety day program and tell her where it came from with the last installment.

After getting her situated she was tired as a slave picking master's cotton in one hundred degree weather. Her night had turned to day; she showered and quickly fell asleep.

The sound of the alarm beeping didn't even wake her. It was the sound of her phone. It was her appointment she was late. She was supposed to be meeting the relator to purchase a building in the Johns Creek area for the second restaurant. This didn't look good because she was to sign the contract and get the deed today. She had already been having a hard time with the caucasian owners they wanted to sell it to the Asians but Daya had money just as long as theirs. She phoned Booker T and asked him to stall them she knew that traffic would be hell and it was going to take her a while to get there. He phoned for a limousine and took them all to lunch at Stoney River's. Booker T was always such a lifesaver. He was always keeping her butt out of the line of fire. She hastily showered, got dressed and headed to the restaurant. On the ride there she checked her phone she had seventeen missed calls and four voice messages. Several calls from an unknown number, a call from Ta-Ta, Margo, Brandy and Mia. Now was not the time to be returning calls or giving details from last night she needed to get to her appointment and quick. The phone rung it was Ta-Ta he was just calling to check up on her and to tell her that Trisha had contacted him at the school to tell him "Thank you".

Daya thought to herself that damn girl is always up to something and how did she get to use the phone. She would deal with that later, that was not her focus right now. She made it to the restaurant in record time. Booker T had gotten everybody super drunk and they were ready to seal the deal. She would began renovations this week and would be opening in the next two months.

Flowers In My Garden

After Papa died and possible went to heaven Mama Sugar would have little men friends as she would call them. She would always say "Baby men are like flowers in a garden. You can have as many as you can handle. Some are seasonal, annuals and some are permanent. You never know which one its going to be. You know you gotta let time decide. Always remember you can't let your garden get over grown and full of weeds. You gotta know when its time to prune, dig up the old and replace them with something new. You also gotta be careful what you plant."

Daya sat in the kitchen looking out her window at the beautiful scenery. It was though she was sitting there having a conversation with Mama Sugar like old times. Things with her had been so complicated lately, when she started trying to make sense of everything she just got even more confused. Light had seemed to be her everything her all in all, her one and only, but a lifetime commitment with him both excited her and frightened her. She wondered why is it that when you get everything you always wanted you don't really want when you have it.

She began to wonder if she was walking around with a sign on her forehead that read:" I'm available." because she was attracting so many men the brothers and the others. Sitting there she began to sort the flowers in her garden. She decided that her life needed a little pruning.

She decided she needed to go over to the house to check on it. She would go by every now and then. Being that the house was built on love she was always seemed relaxed there. It was her dream homesbuilt for her by her dream man. Her dreamed had crumbled around her but she was sure to pick up the pieces.

Light had decided not to sell the house in hopes of them rekindling what they once had. She kept her key. He told her that the house was hers as long as she wanted it. She couldn't stay there because it just didn't feel right without him. She pulled up in the circular brick paved drive way, put her car in park, turned off the ignition, Sat there for about fifteen minutes before she decided to go inside. The lawn was immaculate the ferns were arranged on the porch where she left them, the rocking chairs that they would sit in at night brought back memories. She took a deep breath unlocked the door and went in. Everything was in its proper place, just seemed like she was returning home. That was what it felt like to her home. She walked around and admired every room. Standing in the kitchen window she looked out at the lake and smiled when she thought about the picnic Light had for her out there one day. She went into the living room to get her bottled water out her purse when she heard the noise of someone trying to unlock the door. She panicked, and then remembered that only four people had a key. She glanced out the window and she saw Light's black Range Rover. It was him. The door opened before she could blink. There he was live and in the flesh looking better than ever. He stood in the door way. Their eyes locked and bucked like a dear in head lights. He was dressed in all white linen shirt, pants, white baseball cap, white air-force ones, his diamond encrusted platinum cross hung on the outside of his shirt. His ribbed wife beater peeped out his shirt. Fresh from the barber shop chair, his Go-t was lined and trimmed perfectly. Carmex glistened on his lips. His lean, tall, muscular frame hung the outfit picture-perfect like he was a manikin in a store on display.

Uncertain about what to say they both spoke simultaneously.

"Um sorry didn't know you were going to be here."

Daya picking up her purse. " No don't leave I will."

She brushed passed him and the scent of her detained him. He couldn't resist the way the long black cotton halter dress hugged her hips, her coco- brown shoulders glimmering gave her a sexy look. He grabbed her in his arms and kissed her. She didn't fight at all, it was as rivers of honey flowed from his mouth into hers. She was lifeless and he breathed life into her. They exchanged soul tales. That which only soul-mates could do. She enjoyed the strength of his hands on her back. He slid his hands up under her dress and rubbed her from front to back inside and out. She loved every minute of his touch. She unbuttoned his pants to feel his man hood and it greeted her with cheer. She stroked and massaged him, until she wanted to feel him inside of her. He lifted her to him placed his back up against the door bent his knees in a chair sitting position so that she could feel all of him and he all of her. He bent her over the sofa, spread her legs and tasted her blackberry jam enjoying every lick. Their hearts beat fast and uninterrupted like that of a cardiac work-out.

He carried her to the kitchen still inside of her placed her on the island and enjoyed another taste. She wanted badly to return the favor and she placed him in her mouth he melted like warm chocolate and enjoyed every stroke of her wet mouth on him. He wanted to explode, but had to get one more feel of her inside. Her entered her gently and she tightened herself around his manhood he exploded long and hard. She enjoyed the look of pleasure on his face. They washed up and retired to the family room without mumbling a word and fell asleep wrapped in each others arms. Sometimes things are better left unsaid. She woke to find him dressed and gone so she thought. When she sat up there was Amber sitting on the fireplace with a gun pointing at her.

Startled. She jumped! "Oh my goodness what are you doing her?"

"No bitch! What are you doing here fucking my damn husband?" She stood up and walked towards Daya. " I thought I told you that if I ever caught you with him. I was going to kill you and make it look like suicide. You done fucked with the wrong one. But I guess you wanted to try your luck and see if I was playing. Well say your prayers whore." She cocked the gun and put it to Daya's head. Daya spoke in a calm voice " Look Amber, let's talk about this."

She nudged Daya's head with the gun. "There is nothing to talk about!" she said raising her voice an octave louder. Then Daya pushed her and tripped her. The gun fell to the floor. Daya dove for her and started getting the best of her. "Bitch you aint shit without that gun.

Meanwhile Light detoured back to the house because he remembered that he and Daya did not talk and he did not want to leave that way. When he pulled up in the drive way he saw Ambers' car. He threw his truck in park phoned his father and Doe and ran in the house. He rushed through the door damn near walking threw it. He witness Daya putting a whooping on Amber. He chuckled and broke them up. "Light no!" Daya screamed. Amber dove for the gun. They got into a scuffle a shot was fired. All three of them hit the floor. Daya crawled to her purse to retrieve her phone to call 911. She gave the operator the information and blanked out for a few seconds. When she came to herself she saw Light on the floor covered in blood moaning. She ran to his side applying pressure to his womb.

He asked her "Are you alright?"

"No are you alright? don't worry about me." she said.

His eyes were getting weak. His voice was fading.

"Stay with me damit! Stay with me you hear me!"

She cried out to the Lord. "Dear God please save him. It took me too long to find him and a longtime

to realize I love him. Please don't take him away
from me."

In a weak tone he spoke gasping for his breathe " I'm
not going to leave you. You are my everything. I'm
holding on with all that I have. I want leave you
ever."

In that instance Doe and his father entered the door
and the rescue worker were dead in their tracks.

"Collier?" She looked puzzled, surprised and
confused.

"Excuse me. Excuse me." The paramedic told Doe.

The muscular short man examined Light and radioed
for a helicopter. "Who is the next of kin?" he asked
in a very direct and concerned tone.

Collier spoke in his distinctive tone. "He's my son."

"He has lost a lot of blood we've got to life flight
him to the hospital."

Daya looked at Collier then at Light but realized now would not be a good time to ask, but she sure as hell had a lot of questions. Light began to fade in and out of consciousness.

"Stay with damit me. Stay with me!" the paramedic yelled as he applied more pressure to the wound. He was working so hard he was sweating. He was determined to keep Light alive. Daya dropped to her knees and knelt by his side. She took his hand.

" Baby, I need you please just hold-on." She pleaded.

The other paramedic came and they lifted him on the stretcher and took him out the door. The police walked in, surveyed the scene and began to investigate immediately.

Looking around, at that moment Daya realized Amber was gone. With pen and paper in his hand, he questioned her. "Ma'am I'm going to need to ask you a few questions."

"It was three of us here. We got into a struggle over the gun and they both got hit. She threatened to kill me and she was about to until I kicked the gun out of her hand." She pointed in the direction of the trail of blood. Still in shock of what happened she screamed. "Light! Light!. I gotta go!" She ran out the door and saw that the ambulance was about to pull-off she beat on the back door.

"Ma'am look we have an emergency here we gotta go and fast. We have no time to waste." The driver began blowing the horn because the Life flight helicopter was waiting down the road. Light lifted his head and said in a whisper. "That's my wife let her in." The paramedic assisted her he let her in. They sped off. Doe and Collier explained to the police what happened. The police called for backup and they began to search for her.

The helicopter got them to the hospital in record time. The trauma team was ready and waiting for Light to arrive. They rushed him off to surgery. While he was in surgery Collier explain the situation.

He told Daya that he and Light had recently found one another and that they had discussed when would be the appropriate time to tell her. She was calm about the situation the only thing she was worried about was Light. After hours of waiting and praying, the surgeon came to the family waiting room. He could see that they all had an empty look on their faces. "He's fine. The surgery went well. He's one lucky fella that's all I gotta say….He's sumtin' lucky."

Daya took a deep sigh. Her head was pounding from the wait and anxiety. They were all well relieved to hear the new and went to visit him in recovery. The detective from the house came to the hospital to tell them that he was going to have an officer around the clock for Light because they still had not found Light and was sure that she would come back looking to harm him and Daya. He told them about her lengthy criminal and psychiatric record. Day excused herself and made a call to the girls. She planned to go crash at Shayla's, until psycho-mycho Amber was in police custody.

Three days had passed and Light was recovering well. The doctor's were talking of letting him go home sooner than they had expected. There were still no signs of Amber. It was as if she had fell off the face of the earth or dropped dead somewhere. Amber was a smart cookie she had checked herself into the same hospital as Daya Young. She was exactly four rooms down from Light. In her room she plotted and planned on how she was going to end both of their lives. She began to still needles from the supply closest on the third floor and had ordered some medication off-line and had it delivered to her room. Daya was in Lights room around the clock.

It was about three a.m., the eve before Light's discharge from the hospital. Amber had confiscated a nurse scrub uniform and badge from the nurses' locker-room. She had decided that tonight would be the night she took Light out. She had made up her mind, If he didn't want her then he would be with anyone else especially Daya. She could tell from seeing them together and how he looked at her that they were really in love and that she was the only thing stopping them from being together. She entered the room Light laid in the bed sleeping with Daya in the chair by his side. The officer came inside the room. He noticed the photo on her employee badge wasn't her. And that she closely resembled the photo of the person they were looking for. He called for back-up on his radio.

She entered the room surveyed the scene and walked over to Light's bedside. She retrieved the prefilled contaminated syringe from her front pocket. This poisonous concoction was sure to take him out quickly. The officer caught her just as she was about to inject it into Light's I.V.

"Excuse me nurse the charge nurse would like to see you." He said looking at her as if he knew what she was up to. "Thank you give me a minute I'll be right there let me give this med." She said breaking into a sweat.

The officer stepped in her direction and she dropped the syringe and quickly picked it up. At that moment the other officers' busted in the room with their weapons drawn. "Ma'am we know who you are now step away from the patient with your hands up." All the commotion startled Light and Daya. Daya sat up and looked around to see what was happening right before eyes. Amber was trapped with no place to run. She was cornered and outnumbered. She took the coward way out and injected herself. She fell to the floor had a seizure and took her last breath. Everyone in the room was shocked. No one expected that outcome.

The incident was a bit much for Light to handle, he went into cardiac arrest. Daya stood to his side her knees buckled. She hit the floor. The medical professionals began to resuscitate him. He was not responding. They rushed him out of the room. Daya ran alongside them as they rushed him to the Intensive Care Unit. He came too for a brief moment and motioned for Daya. "Yes baby?" she said leaning close to him for his words were very faint.

"Joy. Joy take care of my baby girl for me please. Promise?" he said then he rested his eyes.

Double Duty

It had been three months and Daya's world had been turned completely upside down. On this particular day she was nursing a serious migraine. Joy was teething and was very irritated. The nanny had a family emergency and was unable to come. Brandy turned party planner was calling with her one hundred baby shower demands. Trisha was scheduled to get out of rehab. Mia had a date and had asked her a week earlier to babysit. She had a "To Do List" ten miles long and not enough hours or time in the day to even get started. Not to top it off she was well into planning the Grand-Opening for "Suga's 2", but the construction company had to stop construction for a while because they had illegal aliens working. If it wasn't one thing then it was a thousand.

The sound of the phone ringing was actually a sigh of release for her because it took her mind off the two ton truck that she was caring around. It was Artise he was calling to inform her that he got the chair covers that Brandy wanted for the shower. He was working every detail out to the fullest. If it wasn't for him she would have already been a sunken ship.

"Hey Girl! Are we still on for drinks?" he asked in his cheerful perky voice. Not even aware of what the time was Daya was frazzled and dazzled.

"Drinks?" She said holding her head. "Oh! Shesh! I forgot. Honey I got kids and you name it going on over here. I'm sorry I can't make it. I need a rain check." He could hear her desperate cry. He was always a life saver and could always put out a fire except for the one in his pants.

"Honey I'll be there in ten." He said then hung up the phone. He phoned for back up. He called Candi and Shayla.

She was ever so thankful for him. Trying to tidy up the place before he came, but was overwhelmed.

Team Rescue arrived in record time. Looking her over Artise said "Girl you look a mess." The other two nodded in agreement. They wisped passed her and left her standing at the door. She was usually the leader of the rescue team, but this day she was in need. She realized that it was okay to need help and that asking for help didn't make her helpless. She was so grateful because they brought calmness to the madness. They came in willing and ready to work. They cooked, clean and entertained the kids while she relaxed in the tub. Shayla brought her a glass of wine.

Knocking on the door. "Can I come in for a sec? I got my eyes closed."

She laughed. "Yes. Silly girl."

She opened the door. "Here! girl look like you need this bad." She said handing her a glass of Mascato.

"Thanks girl. You're the best."

The time away gave plenty of time to meditate and organize her thoughts. She was able to regroup and balance the circus that was going on around her. Looking around and seeing that none of this would have been possible without them, she felt a great sense of appreciation. Although the enemy was trying to tear her down with all sorts of distractions, GOD was still in control. He had surrounded her with good friends that loved her and didn't mind coming to her rescue.

Changing Lanes

Mia had become a mother and somebody's significant other faster than she anticipated. Things had ended really peacefully between her and Kathy. Although, Kathy had left kind of foul, by sneaking around with her ex-husband. She wasn't really sweating it. She didn't feel the raft of the break-up because Olivia came into her life. Although she wasn't really feeling ole boy like that at this point; He was good conversation and a warm body in the bed every weekend. She wasn't alone and that was the point. He did have a lot of good qualities. He had a successful career and enjoyed spending time with her as well as entertaining her. He wasn't her Knight in shining Armor, but he would do for the time being. He also cared enough to consider relocating to the same city so that they could have a closer relationship. She was trying to take it slow, but it seemed that things were progressing pretty fast.

She had a lot of hang-ups from being with Howard and was trying to avoid any pit falls. She enjoyed the weekend visits with him. It was always something to look forward to on Friday's. As much as she professed not to have feelings for him, they were undeniably establishing. She had got to the point where she anticipated his arrival on Fridays and dreaded his departure on Monday's. Besides he was indeed a fun person and real good company. He had even brought his son Kevin one weekend to meet them. He treated him and Olivia to a weekend on the town kiddie style they went to the Georgia Aquarium, Dave and Busters, Malibu and the Atlanta Zoo. Kevin and Olivia hit it off pretty well and questioned if they were brother and sister.

Two back to back bad relationships were enough for her. She wondered if she was being too carefree with him. She had decided that she would create her own happiness and if that included him, then so be it. Her business was thriving and she was loving motherhood. Love was not on her agenda, but Rylan was planning to nippily sweep her off her feet.

Mia walked into the restaurant glowing with a big smile on her face. She was so happy to see Daya considering what she had been through. Daya greeted her with a warm hug. They sat and waited for the rest of the gang. They did some catching up and teased one another. They were interrupted by Daya's cell phone ringing.

"Chick where are you? With your slow ass..." Daya said in a joking tone. Shayla paused and didn't come back in her normal playful tone. That was not like Shayla to get back with her. Daya got serious and asked. "Are you ok girl?"

Scott's ex-wife had her blocked in his drive-way and refused to move. Shayla was by no means intimidated but phoned her to let her know the reason for her tardiness.

"Hey girl! Imma be a few minutes late, this trick white tramp done lost her mind. She must not know who I am." Shayla said in a not so calm tone.

"Wait...wait! What happened?"

"Oh Scott's ex-wife is over here and has my car blocked in. I asked her to move and so did he. He is trying not to make a scene and is being way to kind to her. So give me a few. I gotta handle this."

"Ok. No not by yourself give me the address we are on the way."

Meanwhile Mia was taking it all in. She phoned Candi and gave her the heads-up and told her to meet us there.

Daya phoned Ta-Ta gave him the address and told him she needed to have a car towed at this address. He dispatched the driver and in no time he was in route.

Finishing the call Daya looked at Mia. "What?" Daya said in a very sweet tone trying to look innocent, as if she had done nothing wrong.

"You crazy! I hope you know that. Right?" Mia said, with a sinister jovial laugh.

"Yeah I know! At least I'm not afraid to admit it." She assumed that it was ok to be a little out of the loop. She really was a calm person, but don't mess with her family or friends because you were sure to meet her evil twin. Daya told Mia what was going down and she out of nowhere found some backbone and got so hyped about the situation Daya had to calm her down. Mia was so passive. People always walked over her. She never stood up for herself. In college Daya had to come to her rescue on many occasions. Daya paid for the wine and tipped the server. They headed to Scott's house, speeding down GA 400 and made it there in record time. They pulled up into his driveway in front of his Italian style mansion. Parked very close behind Shayla's convertible red Porsche was a champagne

Escalade. They could see a silhouette of a female in the driver seat, but wasn't sure who it was. Mia got out the car, walked to the front door and rang the doorbell. She looked back noticing that Daya was not behind her. Daya took her time. She sat there, in her car for a moment to get her thoughts together, because she knew that she was not responsible for her actions. She got out the car and walked up to the driver side of the truck and tapped on the window. The female sitting in the truck, looked straight at Daya threw the dark tinted driver side window and ignored her. Rolling her eyes she didn't acknowledge Daya's presence at all. Daya tapped again, but this time much harder. The passenger in the truck rolled down the window. There she was sitting in the truck with a stupid look on her face. She turned beet red at the sight of Daya. She wasn't much to look at. A petite unnatural blonde. Looking like a spoil little brat. From her demeanor you could tell that she was used to getting things her way, but today was not one of them. She must have grown balls to come over like this and try and check somebody.

"Is there a problem here?" Daya asked. She looked at Daya up and down as if she was sizing her up. "No, but its going be if you don't get your ass away from my truck bitch."

Before she knew it Daya had grabbed her by her hair and began to pull her out the truck so fast, Mrs. Bad as I Wanna Be did not even have time to respond. It was as if lightning struck. Mia, Scott and Shayla came running out of the house. Daya told her " Oh I got your bitch..bitch."

They pulled them apart. Ta-Ta's driver Butch pulled up with the tow truck. Shayla, Scott and the ex-wife were all looking puzzled. The ex-wife ran to the truck and Daya motioned for him to move the truck. Butch was straight from the hood, he hooked that truck up so faster than a New York minute and towed it, down the hill out of the way with her inside hollering and screaming hysterically like a mad lady.

They all looked at Daya in disbelief. She adjusted her shirt and looked backed in innocence. "What?

Don't nobody have time to be playing with her. Scott you need to check her."

"Yeah you do!" rolling her neck and late as usual Candi replied, then asked "Now what happened?"

They all just busted out laughing. Because she was a stone trip. Always late for everything.

He was so mellow that her antics didn't faze him he was use to her temper tantrums and drama. The neighbor had informed her that he was dating some black chick and that she was probably a stripper. The neighbor wrote down Shayla's tag number and gave it to her. She quickly discovered who she was and that she had two practices. Kinsley was her name she and Scott met in college their families were very good friends and from the same elite group. Their parents had been trying to get them to date since high school, but he was not interested in her. Her mother coached and groomed her on the premise that she needed to marry money. She knew that his family had plenty of it. They had a short courtship and married after college. Love and happiness were not a part of the relationship. Scott did not like living in misery. He divorced her and gave her a settlement, but she was not too happy about that. She especially could not handle losing her husband to a black woman. She had become the talk of the social club. Scott on the other hand, was the happiest he had ever been in his life dating Shayla and she too was in the heavens these days. He was a total 360 from Bruce "the scum-bag". He genuinely cared about her and showed it in more ways than one. Their relationship was bourgeoning into something beautiful. He respected and treated her like the queen she was. Against his parents' wishes he dated outside his race and for once in his life was experiencing true love. Something he never felt, not even from his parents. His mother was all about the dollar and her image and his dad was into booze and all the women he could get. Rumor had it that he was sneaking around with this black woman in Decatur and that he had her set-up nice. He gave her a monthly stipend. Her house, car and all were paid for.

Daya apologized to Scott for the incident in the driveway. He kindly accepted and the girls headed for their lunch and spa date. Brandy called to see where they were and what was taking them so long. Just as she phoned they walked into the restaurant. Daya explained what had went down and she wanted to know why no one had called her.

"Look you are seven months pregnant honey. What are you going to do besides go into labor?"

They all laughed uncontrollably. After a very satisfying and filling dinner, they left the restaurant and headed to the spa.

At the spa the subject of Trisha came up. Her presence was kinda missed, but not much considering how annoying she could be always thinking everything is about her. She would be coming home in a week now. For the first time in her life she had a job that was a requirement for the program. She was working in the medical records department at the hospital. It was hard to believe that she was actually going to somebody's job. Trisha didn't have a job in high school or college. While everyone else was working to earn extra money she was somewhere acting like Elizabeth Taylor or Paris Hilton and she was nobody's heiress. Her parents didn't want her to work, they just wanted her to focus on her studies. It didn't help because she still got pregnant. They handicapped her giving her everything she asked for and by sheltering her. She didn't have any life skills. Poor thing couldn't balance a checkbook, wash her own clothes or nothing. College was a true culture shock to her, She got buck wild. She thought that all men were going to spoil her like her daddy and that is what she searched for.

Daya was such a true friend. She had kept her house and bills current for her while she was away in the program. She still had not told Trisha about the money that Mr. Marvin had given her to put away for her. She knew that she would blow every single red cent. She had no accountability or responsibility for anything not even her son. She was all about herself. He lived with his father's mother. As soon as she found out about the money she would sure quit that job and run through the money like water. Daya wasn't even certain if she would ever tell her, she decided that she would just make monthly deposits into her account and make her think that Mr. Marvin had it set up that way.

Kathy had landed a new job with the government. She and Mitchell were inseparable. She said that she had a new respect for their relationship. It was fresh and it was revitalizing. It was a new found love. She said that the first time around she didn't appreciate him like she should have. He allowed her to take advantage of him and catered to her every need. He had become her doormat. Now things were totally different, he stood his ground and carried his weight. He still catered to her but was not so much at her beck and call. She no longer treated him like a little boy, but the man that he was. Mitchell had come from a family of women. He was his mother's only son and the brother of two younger sisters. He assumed the role of nurturer at an early age. His mother treated him like he was her husband and he tried his best to live up to that role to his sisters as well. So when he met over bearing Kathy he was right at home, because that is what he was used too. Mitchell was indeed a good man, there was no doubting that. Kathy finally realized that and focused more on his attributes rather than his faults. She was growing and evolving into a mature individual.

Light had successfully recovered and completed his rehab. Daya had loved him back to good health. She had poured all she knew into him to help him and refused to handicap him. These days she was pretty exhausted being a surrogate to his daughter, seeing after him and Trisha, while running the restaurant and trying to oversee the construction on the new restaurant. She was sure she loved Light, there was no doubt about that, but all the recent events were stressing her to the point of separation from him. It was noticeable and he was feeling alienated, but was not going to let that be a stumbling block for them. He would do everything in his power to reconnect with her and get things back on track. Light always had something up his sleeve. Daya was the love of his life and he aimed to please her. He phoned his travel agent to assist him with his plans.

He's Back

Light was truly the man no doubt. When he did something he did it big. Especially, when it came to Daya. The trip to the Bahamas would be a great get away for them. A chance for them to renew, relax and reconnect. Shoot he was hoping that they would make a baby, but that is not all he'd planned to pull out his hat. He was like a magician full of surprises you just never knew what he was up too. He was not a predictable individual. He always had one up on you.

That morning Daya had left the house with her panties in a knot. It was visible that the stress was getting to her. She had to stop construction on the building because the contractor had illegal aliens working for him. So this would delay the Grand-

Opening by three weeks. This was so far off her target date. Trisha had a setback, got caught sleeping with the therapist and was required to do another four weeks at a facility in Brunswick, GA on top of that Artise had taken ill. Daya had literally become a walking steam-pot ready to blow at any minute. Light was certain that he would not let that happen to his woman. He would come to her rescue pronto.

The trip to Nassau, Bahamas was just what she needed and he knew it. It was Wednesday afternoon. He had made sure her schedule was clear. Light had asked her to go for a ride with him. He thought it was going to be hard because she was kind of moody. She cheerfully agreed, which made things very easy. He convinced her to let him blind fold her and drove to the airport. When the car stopped she was anxious to remove the blind fold. The suspense was killing her. He was tickled silly because she was so antsy like a kid at Christmas. He got out the car and went around to her side opened the door, helped her out the car, grabbed her hand and said "Walk with me baby."

Shaking her head. "Oh heck no. When do I get to take this thing off? Where are you taking me?"

Laughing he asked, "What you don't trust me? Come on baby. You know I got you. Just trust me on this one. Relax."

When they got to the front of the airport, he removed the blindfold.

"We're going to the Bahamas for a couple of days."

"I have business to tend to."

"I've put everything on hold for you until, you get back."

She just looked at him. It was just like him to have everything already taken care off. He knew she would not want to leave with so many irons on the fire. They boarded the flight and sat in their first-class seats.

They arrived in the beautiful Bahamas island. The driver greeted them at the airport and drove them to the resort. In the backseat they rode in silence and snuggled up with one another. After thinking about it maybe a vacation was what she needed. Just the sight of the water was relaxing. Light felt the tension leaving from her body as she loosened up and started to unwind. He kissed her on the forehead.

The resort was breath taking, equipped with every amenity imaginable. The houseman Jonathan greeted them and advised that he and his assistants would be taking care of all their needs for the week. Light shook his hand "Pleased to meet you Jonathan."

"Likewise Sir. Your luggage. Do you have any?"

"No, we are going to be needing, toiletries and everything." Light wrote down their sizes and handed it to him.

He made a phone call to the front desk to have them bring swimwear and clothing for them. Daya made a dash for the beach. She kicked off her shoes, stepped out on the screened patio and ran to the beach. The gorgeous pristine view of the Atlantic was breath taking. She enjoyed feel of the powdery white sand between her toes. She stood at the shore and let the shore wash her feet. It felt that everything she was caring was floating out into the sea. Inhaling the fresh pure air, she stretched her arms to the heavens. From the patio Light adored her and decided not to disturb her.

The butler walked up to him handing him a drink. "Rum Punch Mr. Lightfoot for you and the lady?" He pointed to Daya. He walked on the beach.

"For you Mrs. Lightfoot? Enjoy! May I provide you anything else." He asked as he placed chilled bottled water and the tray of assorted fresh fruits on the table. He laid white towels on the back of the mocha wicker chairs, opened the umbrella on the table.

"Thank you." She said smiling showing her appreciation.

The assistant admired her beauty and humbleness.

"My pleasure." He said.

. Light couldn't resist it any longer. He stepped off the patio onto the sand snuck up behind her, wrapped his arms around her waist, kissed her on the neck then nibbled on her ear. She turned and thanked him for his kind gesture and told him how much she appreciated.

"You know you never cease to amaze me. Your timing couldn't have been better." She told him.

"Only the best for you. Only the best." He responded nodding his head.

Back inside the villa the chef prepared a feast for them, some of their favorites with an island twist. Looking through the clothes they shopped like little kids. They modeled different outfits for one another. Finally they picked their clothes for the rest of the trip showered and headed out for a night on the island. Their first night there was magical. This was a great way for them to reunite. With Amber out of the way Light felt that he was no longer a prisoner in his own world, she could no longer threaten his and Daya's life and that they could finally be together. He was ready to move on with his life and make it complete. He tossed and turned all that night. He was nervous and anxious, uncertain of how Daya would respond to his next surprise. He got up and went to the beach and prayed. After his prayer he felt a sense of relief. He was sure he had made the best decision he had ever made in his life. He phoned Brandy to double check to make sure he doctor had cleared her to fly. He called Shayla to see if she and Scott would make the flight. She told him that she had got a replacement for the office and they would be on the flight. Kathy would bring Joy, Margo and the rest were all aboard, ready, excited and would be there in a couple of hours.

Daya awoke to the sunlight peeping through the white wooden blinds and the smell of the breakfast being prepared in the kitchen tickling her nose. Stirring around in the bed she finally got up, washed up, slipped on her robe and skipped to the kitchen to find Light giving the chef tips on how to prepare her omelet. Standing back she listened and admired how he knew exactly how she liked her food. She laughed to herself. She snuck up behind him at the breakfast bar, putting her hands over his eyes.

"Hey U!" he said taking her hand and putting it in his.

"You got up early huh? Why didn't you wake me?" She said holding her head slightly tilted to the side, looking curious.

"You were sleeping so beautifully and peacefully. I didn't want to disturb you. Besides I have a few things I'd like to do today." He replied resting his arm on her lower back, then followed up with a pat on her butt.

They enjoyed a scrumptious breakfast. Afterwards they lounged on the beach. Daya walked to the shore to wet her feet and noticed to the right of her a crew setting up for a wedding. Admiring the decorations she called to Light to come view it as well.

He commented. "That's nice huh?"

"It's better than nice it's incredible." She continued to look and watch every detail.

"That's kinda what you wanted huh?" Smiling he turned his head in the other direction.

"Yeah! Yeah! It's exactly what I wanted. Wow they are doing a great job."

His cell phone rung and he stepped away to take the call. It was the tailor they had arrived with the items Light had requested. Light went inside the villa to find that the full staff was there and ready for them. He called out to Daya she came in with a confused looked on her face. He asked the staff for a moment. He and Daya stepped into the room. His heart was racing, but he spoke with confidence.

Taking a deep breath, he took her hand placing it in his and looked dead into her brown eyes. "The bible tells us that he who finds a wife finds favor with the Lord. I'm ready to inherit my favor. I want you as my wife. I cannot live another day on this earth with out you as my wife. I want you in my life for ever. And our forever starts today baby. The wedding you saw being setup that's ours. I made all the arrangements. The staff is here to help us get dressed. Our family and friends are here to attend the ceremony. They got here this morning."

Her mouthed dropped and her heart dropped to her stomach. "Are you serious? I can't believe you. Oh my goodness. My hair? Nobody touches my hair but Toinette." Daya tried to make an excuse because she had come to realize that Light was what she wanted but not what she needed, but she had to make a decision and fast.

"She's here waiting for me to call." He phoned the driver to bring her over. "So what do you say?"

This brought chills all over her body. She was stuck. She loved him and knew that he loved her and that they could have a good life together. But she was afraid. The moment was here. She had played this moment over and over in her head, but never thought it would come. He stood there with his eyes fixated on her. She had gotten comfortable with things as they were besides she had been thinking about Keynan lately and was going to call him when they got back. Her life flashed before her. She could not believe that he had arranged all this. She didn't see this one coming. He had chartered a flight for family and friends to attend the wedding for the day because some would be leaving after the reception. He had her three favorite gowns, shoes and accessories. He left no stone unturned all bases were covered. Thinking back to when she was a little girl, she always said that she wanted to get married on the beach and that she wanted a lot of pretty flowers, white chairs, tiki-torches and the chiffon fabric blowing in the ocean breeze. Just like she had seen outside. It was a dream come true.

She walked down the sandy isle to the vocals of R&B singer Joe. He was amazing. The ceremony was simply breath taking. Everything was in its proper place. Brandy, Mia, Shayla, Candi and Kathy made the prettiest bridesmaids. Candi and Mia's daughter's Christina and Olivia were the flower girls. They all cried when they saw her. She looked like a real princess. She was beautiful, a gorgeous site to see. They exchanged their vows right before the sunset. The fish aquarium dance floor was an instant hit. The exotic cuisine and many ice sculptures were superb. Everyone enjoyed themselves eating and dancing the night away. It was unbelievable to see that he had pulled all that together on such short notice. Light was surely the "Make it Happen Man", a title much fitting and deserving for him, everyone around him knew it. Some admired him for it and the haters envied him. It didn't bother him because he was a man of his word. Sitting back observing and taking all the festivities in he beamed with joy. For the first time in his life he was happy and felt a sense of completeness. He knew that God had truly blessed him with the best. He felt the wedge growing between them and decided it was a now or never situation. He chose now. For him this day couldn't have been any more perfect. He had his father that he had searched for, for many years by his side. He had married the girl of his dreams and had a beautiful daughter.

The trip ended early when Daya got a call that Artise had taken a turn for the worst. She had to rush to his side. The pneumonia was affecting both lungs and his organs were shutting down. Frank let her speak with him she told him, "Tise you better hold your ass on and I mean it literally. Hold your ass on till I get there. I'm flying out first thing in the morning. I love you meat head."

He was weak and his voice was faint, but managed to laugh at her and crack a joke. "Imma hold my ass on 'til you get here honey, but you better hurry up. You know I don't have much."

She laughed, but tears rolled down her face. She could hear it in his voice. She asked Light to phone the pilot to see if they were able to leave. He advised that the visibility was poor and that it would not be safe. Morning could not come fast enough; she tossed and turned all night. Light was by her side comforting her. The sound of Joy crying woke them, they dressed, went to the airport and the Lightfoot's headed home to Atlanta.

Sunshine and Rain

As promised Artise waited for Daya to arrive, shortly after her arrival he passed away. She was thrilled to know that he made it back to see him and lead him to Christ. She was satisfied knowing that he accepted the invitation. Moments later Brandy went into labor. The wedding and a death within twenty-four hours was enough to send anyone into labor. It was good everybody got to see him. Frank was one sad puppy. He planned a very nice home-going service and put him away just as he would have wanted "in style." Artise always said he wanted to give them something to talk about when he was alive and he sure as hell wanted to leave them something to talk about when he was dead and gone.

Twenty eight hours later Brandy became a proud mother, giving birth to a beautiful baby girl. She looked like a minnie Brandy. Brandy's movie was released and hit the top of the charts which gave her a lot of notoriety as an actress. Her pregnancy photos were published in a local magazine. She received an offer to do a fitness DVD. She launched her modeling studio and dominated the fashion world with her models.

Trisha came home from rehab. You would have thought she would've been thankful for Daya keeping everything in order for her. She didn't even let her know that she had been released, the counselor called Daya and told her that she signed herself out. For some reason she had a hang-up with Daya. Maybe she thought that Light told her that she tried to push up on him and the guilt was killing her. Unlike the many others she was not able to seduce him. She put the house up for sale, sold all the furniture, emptied her bank account and left town.

Shayla and Scott got engaged. He gave her a stunning five carat diamond ring in titanium setting. Shortly after they decided to move-in his condominium on Peachtree Street together and planned to marry in six months. He finally introduced her to his parents and surprisingly they were very receptive. They gave her a warm welcome to the family. His mother even invited her for tea at the country club. This was a major step, but Scott was proud. He and Light became business partners.

Mia continued her long distance relationship with Rylan. This seemed to work best for them at the present. They saw each other every other weekend, spent every holiday as a family, Olivia and Kevin enjoyed the summers together. Mia had Kathy to relinquish her rights so that he could legally adopt her. Mia auditioned and became a guest host on a popular home design show for a season.

Kathy got a promotion. She ran for political office and conceded her opponent. She and Mitchell successfully conceived.

Margo moved in Brandy's building to help her with the baby. She met and married her a younger man.

The real estate makert went sour and so did Candi's finances. She had rental properties, but couldn't keep tenants. She decided to sale some of the properties and go back to school for nursing. She and Christina downsized to one of her properties. Chrsitina got a modeling contract with Brandy and Candi worked for Daya part-time. She finally caught up with her dead beat baby daddy and he started paying child support. She thought that her life was over because selling houses was all she knew, but found that life was just beginning. She met an older gentleman and they fell in love.

Daya and Light built a new home in Dunwoody. The second restaurant and was doing pretty well. Daya devoted her time to raising Joy and her magazine. Light continued to treat her like a queen. Light became a dedicated husband, father and business man. He joined Daya's church. He spent more time at home. He developed a great relationship with his father. Daya launched

"Y-Mag" a women's magazine. She gave each of the women in her life a column: Brandy (fitness and beauty), Shayla (health), Mia (style and fashion), Kathy (political views), Candi (Mom and Me) Margo had a column named: "Mother's Knows Best" and Daya wrote on finances. The magazine is circulating throughout the country and is expected to go international.

They all got the life they so deserved and desired. Like Dear Ole Mama Sugar would say "Your life is what you make it. In this life you can sink or swim. I'm not going to promise you that everyday is going to be all rosy. No you gonna have some ups and downs. Life gone bring you some disappointments believe that. But one thing for certain baby you don't get stuck on the things that are wrong 'cause they will tear you down. You hold your head-up pray to the Lord above and he will make it alright. You hear me? Find you a man that loves you for who you are. A man that will give you his last, a man that is going to treat your body right and respect yo' mind. Not some fool that gone jump on you humping like a rabbit and you can't even hold a conversation with him. No matter what you stay true to yo 'self. God aint make you no fool. The best thing you can do in life is be a good listener. Listen to what people say and that will tell you what kind of person they are."

Mama Sugar would sit me down on that porch and talk to me for hours. She spoke with love and wisdom. Preparing, shaping, molding and equipping me with the tools to be the best woman I can be.

Book Club Questions:

Who was the detective and how did Daya know him?

What was Brandy's boyfriend name?

Who was Toinette? Where did she work? Who were her assistants?

Was Mia a mother? If so, what was her child's name?

Shayla was involved with who? Where did they meet?

What was Light's daughter name & who was her mother?

Notes:

To the Reader:

I Thank you so much for your love and support. I couldn't do it without you. I hope that you enjoyed this book. Be sure to tell a friend. Please visit my site:

www.yasmineharrison.com

I would love to hear from you.

Happy Reading! Peace and Many Blessings,

Yasmine

Other Titles by Yasmine Harrison Include:

Turning Point (Pt.1)

Still…Poetry Collection

7401911R0

Made in the USA
Charleston, SC
28 February 2011